DEATH ON ACCOUNT

Robbie had been planning a raid on the bank for
months. The alarm system was the main risk.
Each till was equipped with a foot pedal which
triggered a warning within seconds to the main
security network, but before the police could be
summoned, two or three minutes must elapse:
vital ones, and enough. In the years that Robbie
had been at the branch it had never been robbed,
though once a security van leaving with the
wages for a local factory had been held up. At
first he had thought of robbing a different bank,
for he felt loyal to his own and it was a sort of
treachery to plot against it. But he knew the
customs of his own branch; he knew the staff; and
above all, he was so much, by this time, a respected
elder figure that he would never be suspected
when he walked in, just after the raid, and discovered what had happened.

Also available by Margaret Yorke

MARGARET YORKE

Death on Account

ARROW BOOKS

Arrow Books Limited
20 Vauxhall Bridge Road, London SW1V 2SA

An imprint of Random Century Group

London Melbourne Sydney Auckland
Johannesburg and agencies throughout
the world

First published by Hutchinson 1979
Arrow edition 1980
Reprinted 1982, 1987, and 1990

Printed and bound in Great Britain by
Courier International Ltd, Tiptree, Essex

ISBN 0 09 924590 6

I

He heard her key in the door.

The body sprawled on the floor, arms spread, blood seeping from a bullet wound in the head. Two women and a man, frozen in shock, huddled against the wall away from the masked gunman. The dead man lay at their feet; he had been shot first in the stomach and then, when he lay groaning on the ground, in the head.

Robbie could not wait to find out what happened next. He switched channels on the television set and when she came into the room he was apparently absorbed by a current events programme. He did not look away from the screen when she entered.

Isabel, stepping on high heels, crossed the room and adjusted the volume control. She tweaked one of the heavy silk curtains which was not hanging straight.

'Well,' she said. 'I can see you've had a profitable evening.'

Robbie glanced at his wife. He looked at her plump neck, the skin crêpey now, and red, but the flesh solid, and imagined the pneumatic feel of her rounded shoulders under his hands. What would it be like to take that coarse neck between his fingers and squeeze it? He stared at her, imagining the look of incredulous horror that would fill her ice-blue eyes as she realized his intentions: they would start to protrude from their sockets; her face would suffuse with colour and at last she would go limp, fall away from

7

him, be silenced for ever. It would be wonderful.

But none of this happened.

'Yours was obviously a success,' he said. She was still wound up, colour high and cold eyes bright.

'As if you cared,' Isabel replied.

Robbie didn't, but if he could endure her barbs and refrain from planting any of his own, she might soon go up to bed and he would be able to switch the television back to the thriller without missing much of the action.

Isabel Robinson had been supervising a charity fashion show at the Crown Hotel, and when it was over she had spent some time in the hotel bar with the other organizers. She owned a dress shop, Caprice, in Harbington's High Street, and had supplied the garments for the display.

'You'll have got some new customers,' Robbie said. 'And publicity, I dare say.'

'I should hope so. I'd hardly bother, otherwise,' said Isabel. 'Bring in the dresses.'

'But you'll have to take them back to the shop in the morning,' Robbie protested. 'Why not leave them?'

'They might be stolen and they'd certainly get crushed,' said Isabel. 'I never leave stock out at night. You know that.'

So Robbie carried in thirty or more outfits and arranged them around the dining room, some spread across the table and others hanging from the door, while Isabel made herself tea in the kitchen and while the television thriller continued, unseen, upon its way. Then he put Isabel's new Golf car away in the garage and locked it. He brought the keys in and put them on a hook in the kitchen.

Isabel took her tea upstairs. Robbie heard her heavy tread ascending, then the bedroom door closing. He went back to the sitting room and switched channels: the thriller was just ending and he was in time to see a police

8

car halt, tyres screaming. Two policemen sprang from it and raced towards a distant figure fleeing along a quayside. There were shots, a scream, then a splash as a body fell into the water. Robbie's pale face was intent as he watched. Crime didn't pay; the perpetrators were very often caught. But it made exciting viewing.

It was nearly midnight when he went to bed. First he prepared a tray for Isabel's morning tea. By taking this up to her each day, he delayed her arrival downstairs until it was time for him to leave for the bank. He ate his own breakfast in peace, cereal and toast, while watching the birds disporting themselves on the table he had made for them outside the kitchen window. He put crumbs out for them before eating himself; tits, finches, humble sparrows – all were welcome.

He crept upstairs, avoiding the tread that squeaked, and went softly past Isabel's door to the second flight which led to the top floor of their old house. Here Robbie slept in a small bedroom under the eaves. Long ago, when they came to this house, this room had been intended for a baby, but no child had come to occupy it. The room was starkly furnished with a narrow iron bedstead, a painted chair and a chest of drawers. Robbie, when he took it over, had built a wardrobe across one end, with hanging space and shelves inside, and a key; but Isabel never came up here. Robbie had removed himself from the large front bedroom with its twin beds five years ago, when he had flu, saying he did not want to infect Isabel, though she was never ill. He had never moved back, and later, with the help of a plumber friend, he had fitted up a washbasin, lavatory and shower in the second attic room so that now he had his own quarters, independent of Isabel. He had been thinking of getting a portable television set to keep up there too; then he could have watched what he liked. He might have managed to pass whole days without ever seeing Isabel. But it was too late now for that plan; they were to move.

The Robinsons spent few evenings together. Isabel often stayed on at the shop, or went over to the second branch, recently opened in a town twenty miles away and run by her former assistant, Beryl Watson. Sometimes she was away on buying trips. Robbie had a large workshop in the garden of 49 Claremont Terrace, and he spent hours there making furniture; he made tables and chairs, stools and lampstands, and he sold what he made to a shop in the town, but the work took time so that his turnover was small and the profit not great. He was secretary of the Horticultural Society and on alternate Tuesday evenings sang with the Harbington Choral Group. By these means he managed to keep out of Isabel's way most of the time.

Sometimes she gave dinner parties for people she wanted to cultivate: councillors and their wives; other shopkeepers; an occasional customer. Robbie had to be on duty then, as host. Unknown to the guests, he always cooked the dinner. Isabel would accept their praise for the delicious meal and Robbie would smile ironically to himself as they expressed envy of his luck in having married such a cook. He never claimed the credit due to him; that would have added to his humiliation.

Isabel was, in fact, a very good cook, but soon after their marriage she had set about turning Robbie into another. Her capability, and his own inexperience, had brought them together. She was a catering manager with the NAAFI when Robbie was doing his army service. She had trained as a cook and caterer and had taught for a time; then, still unmarried at thirty-three, she had gone abroad with the NAAFI. So long ago, to be unmarried at that age was to be a failure and Isabel meant to acquire a husband at almost any price. She soon noticed the quiet young man with the nice manners, and Robbie found her competence reassuring. He never recalled suggesting that they should marry: one evening, at a dance, he found that he was kissing her – afterwards he was not even sure that this was what had happened, but their lips had met. Then it seemed to be assumed that they would marry. Protesting would have been rude; he let it drift, took some slight initiative with kisses and a little more, and was married. He ignored the crude comments of his companions; true, Isabel was not a willowy blonde, but she was very capable. Robbie, whose mother had died when he was eight, thought that he would be safe with her.

She resigned after they were married, when Robbie's service was over and he went into the bank, and she worked in a hotel for some time, as housekeeper. She always earned more than Robbie, and she saved enough to start the dress shop. Harbington at that time was expanding, and lacked such a shop; because she had innate business sense and a great deal of general experience, Isabel soon understood the market she had entered and the shop became very successful. Robbie, she planned, would become in due time the manager of a branch of the bank, while she would run a chain of shops.

But Robbie had not become manager, and now it was obvious that he never would. Some years ago he was moved from Harbington in a sideways promotion to another branch, sixteen miles away in a suburb of Blewton, a large industrial town. He was the first securities clerk there, a responsible position, and he was unlikely to rise any higher. One of the women cashiers was older than he was, and so was the supervisor, but the rest of the staff, including the manager and the chief clerk, were much younger. Robbie was a failure, and Isabel often told him so. Their comfortable style of living, as she said, was paid for by Caprice.

They had bought 49 Claremont Terrace very cheaply

because it was in a nearly derelict condition. Over the years, doing most of the work himself, Robbie had restored and improved it and now it was worth a lot of money. Isabel said that the area was going down, because several of the houses around had been turned into flats and were occupied by young families with children who played in the street and dropped Coke tins in the gutter. Skateboards had appeared recently as an added hazard. Young men tinkered with motorcycles at weekends, making a noise as they tested the engines and tore up and down what should be a quiet residential road. When a fish-and-chip shop opened on the corner, Isabel decided it was time to go. She had put down a deposit on a new neo-Georgian house at the far side of the town, and 49 Claremont Terrace was for sale.

Robbie did not want to move. He had lived in this house for more than twenty years, and he had personally transformed it from a shabby ruin to a well-kept, spruce residence – the agent's description, and accurate. He had made the garden, nurturing all the shrubs and plants from cuttings and seedlings. He knew most of the neighbours, anyway by sight, and every Sunday Charlie Pearce, aged nine, helped him wash the two cars – Isabel's Golf and his own old 1100. Charlie came to the workshop sometimes, too, and was making a three-legged stool under Robbie's instruction. Before Charlie there had been other boys, and when Charlie grew too old there would have been a young one coming along, a surrogate son for Robbie – almost, by now, a grandson.

Isabel meant to put an end to all this.

The new house was in a development of seven, and there would be no Charlie. Isabel had decreed that in the unfortunate event of some of the neighbours actually breeding, Robbie was not to invite their children to help him. Children were noisy and tiresome. If brought into the house, they left sticky fingermarks everywhere, and might walk with dirty shoes across her new pale carpets.

The former breakfast room at 49 Claremont Terrace was now an office, and here on Saturdays Robbie did the books for Caprice. When Isabel opened the first shop, he had fitted it out, building the partitioned changing cubicles and the display racks. Now, Isabel and her partner could afford a professional shopfitter to design and prepare the second shop and to remodel the original one.

Robbie was not needed, except, like the hangers on the rails in the shops, as a fitment.

As Robbie drove to work the day after Isabel's fashion show, he thought about the television thriller he had been watching the night before. The shooting had taken place in a bank. The robber had not planned his raid with enough care: it was folly to tackle a bank single-handed when there were several customers in it; he should have watched to discover the quietest time in the week and picked that moment for the hold-up.

The quietest time at his branch on the outskirts of Blewton was Wednesday afternoon: half-day closing. Some of the shops paid in their takings at lunchtime, so the tills were well stocked, but there were few withdrawals that afternoon and though two cashiers were nominally on duty, there was usually only one till operating at a time. There would be no problem about leaving a getaway car outside at that time, for the street was always empty then.

Robbie had been planning a raid on the bank for months.

The alarm system was the main risk. Each till was equipped with a foot pedal which triggered a warning within seconds to the main security network, but before the police could be summoned, two or three minutes must elapse: vital ones, and enough. In the years that Robbie had been at the branch it had never been robbed, though once a security van leaving with the wages for a local factory had been held up. At first he had thought of robbing a different bank, for he felt loyal to his own and it was a sort of treachery to plot against it. But he knew the customs of his own branch; he knew the staff; and above all, he was so much, by this time, a respected elder figure that he would never be suspected when he walked in, just after the raid which would take place in his lunch hour, and discovered what had happened.

He had imagined it all many times. He parked, every morning, by the recreation ground which was just round the corner from the bank: five minutes' walk. There was a public lavatory, discreetly screened by laurels, in a corner of the ground, and he would go into it to don his disguise. It was usually empty on Wednesdays, though in the school holidays small boys ran in and out. The raid would have to take place in term time, for its success depended on there being no one around. Its success depended, too, upon a getaway car being easily found. The area around the recreation ground was usually well stocked with parked cars, and Robbie had observed that there were always some with the key left in the ignition. After assuming his disguise, he would steal one of these cars, which he would have already marked down; he would drive it to the bank, walk in and demand the cash from the only till operating, and be away in two or three minutes, round the corner again and back into the lavatory, to emerge as himself with the money concealed in the carrier bag which held his sandwiches. It would not be a greedy raid: he would be content with the haul from one till, so the money would not be bulky to carry.

But a getaway car would never be there on a Wednesday afternoon: the streets were deserted then. So the robbery wouldn't take place. It was just a game, something to think about when confined in his domestic prison.

He was sure he could carry it out without being caught, given the right circumstances: a getaway car available on a Wednesday between one and two o'clock; the bank free of customers, with only one cashier on the counter. And a gun.

2

On the way home from the bank, Robbie stopped quite often at the Star in Birley. It wasn't so much the beer he enjoyed as the company. The innkeeper was a retired naval man who told stories about his foreign travels that were often hard to believe but always gripping, and the regular callers included villagers from the area as well as passers-by like Robbie. When Isabel began her scheme to move house, Robbie had suggested they should move to Birley: it was closer to Harbington than Blewton, so still easy for her to get to Caprice, and no further from the second shop. But Isabel did not want an old, quaint village house; she wanted gas laid on and the urban comforts she was used to and some of these would be lacking in Birley.

One of the people Robbie had got to know during the years when he had been calling at The Star was Wilfred Hunt, a farmer, who dropped in occasionally for a pint. As a boy, Robbie had spent happy months in the country with an uncle and aunt after his mother died, and he enjoyed talking to the farmer. Under the impression that Robbie was unmarried, Wilfred Hunt had, one evening, invited him back for supper. There was hotpot from the Aga cooker, apple pie, home-made bread, and cheese, eaten round the big scrubbed table in the kitchen. Wilfred's wife was a cheerful woman who was used to feeding extra mouths without advance warning, and

Robbie felt easy and relaxed in the friendly atmosphere. He discovered, after the meal, that Wilfred's accounting system was flawed and helped him devise a better way of keeping his records; later, he found a young woman who had once worked in the bank and now, married, acted as a travelling farm secretary, to help him. She came once a week.

The evening after Isabel's fashion show, Robbie called at the Star and found Wilfred in the bar. His wife May was away, looking after their married daughter who had just had her second baby.

Wilfred took Robbie back to the farm for supper. There was cold gammon, a huge piece cooked by May before she left, and Wilfred heated up some thick soup from a big jug in the refrigerator. After they had eaten, the farmer took Robbie out to the yard to look at a cow which was due to calve. The nights were cold, and Wilfred was keeping her in; her box was lined with thick straw, and she smelt warm and sweet, surveying the two men – Robbie incongruous in his business suit – with large, patient eyes. She seemed rather restless and Wilfred thought she might drop the calf soon.

Back in the house, they went into Wilfred's study, a shabby, comfortable room with leather-covered armchairs, Wilfred's big, flat-topped desk, shelves of farm records and documents, and a gun cupboard, glass-fronted, holding Wilfred's shotguns and two rifles.

Tonight the desk was piled with untidy heaps of paper, and Wilfred said that his secretary had been away for a month. She had been ill with flu, which had turned to bronchitis.

'I left everything at first, as I thought she'd soon be back,' said Wilfred. 'But poor girl, she's been quite ill, and it's all accumulated.'

'I'll help you sort it out, if you like,' Robbie offered. 'I could come on Saturday.' He could polish off the books for Caprice first.

Wilfred accepted gratefully.

The fine, cold weather broke by the weekend, and with grey skies overhead a strong wind blew rain in gusts along Claremont Terrace as Isabel made ready to leave the house on Saturday morning. A sheet of newspaper had caught against the gatepost and flapped soddenly.

'Thank goodness we won't be here much longer,' Isabel said. 'If you'd been home at a reasonable hour last night I'd have told you that Bridges and Culver have a firm buyer at last. The contracts should be exchanged quite soon.'

Several times already it had seemed that 49 Claremont Terrace had been sold, but before anything was signed each buyer had withdrawn either because they were unable to get a big enough mortgage or because the sale of another house had broken the chain.

'We'll move next month – at Easter,' Isabel said.

Robbie got her car out of the garage and left it with the engine running, ready for her departure. He always did this on Saturdays, though for the rest of the week she did it herself. Unfortunately she was unlikely to have a fatal accident between Claremont Terrace and Caprice, he reflected, not for the first time. Sometimes, when he topped up her car with water or checked the tyres, fantastic plans went through his head, but he knew he would never carry any of them out.

He might rob the bank, though, to prove to himself that he was capable of some immense gesture of rage, though no one else would ever know.

He was to lose his home. He would miss Charlie, his car polisher, and he would miss Darcy's, the shop on the corner where he went for the Sunday papers and where he bought toffees for Charlie and peppermint lumps for himself. He would miss the girls – the bright young women who lived in the street and walked along it in their tight, faded jeans and skimpy sweaters, looking, Isabel said, like tramps, but to Robbie very appealing. Their husbands and boyfriends wore jeans too, and some had long, curling hair, but they were all friendly and would chat to Robbie and Charlie on Sundays as they washed the cars in front of the house.

Upstairs in his room, Robbie had a drawerful of toys with which he rewarded Charlie for his work – not every week, or he would come to expect it, but now and then. Robbie bought some, if he was near a toyshop with time to spare, and others he got by collecting the tops from cereal packets when there was a special offer. Doing this amused him. There was a handsome fire engine in the drawer at the moment, waiting for Charlie.

He thought about defying Isabel over the house. But she had paid off the mortgage; legally she could command control of most of the proceeds from the sale. It would be very difficult, and even if he did it, she could go ahead on her own; she was making enough.

He could refuse to go with her. He could set up on his own. But he knew he would not: he was so accustomed to being her shadow, to taking the easiest way.

He put the breakfast things in the dishwasher in the high-ceilinged kitchen where he had built all the cup-boards. Then he went into the office and got out Caprice's books. The accounts were soon done; Isabel's system with dockets and ledgers at both the shops was strictly enforced and the various assistants, most of them part-timers who each did a day, or even only a half-day, were meticulous about every entry. Then he set off for Birley.

On a Saturday morning it took some time to drive the

length of Harbington's High Street, for people came from miles around to shop there. Cars were double parked, pedestrians, prams and pushchairs poured over the crossings in a long stream. But today, because of the cold weather, there were fewer shoppers than usual, and the trim forms of the young mothers were hidden under bulky jackets.

Robbie reached Wilfred's house soon after eleven o'clock. There was no one about, and the Land-Rover was absent from the yard, so he let himself into the unlocked house through the back door and went through to the study. The mounds of paper were even taller than they had been a few days earlier, and Robbie worked on them for over an hour without interruption, sorting accounts and filing letters, making a pile of bills to be paid.

Pausing for a moment, his glance fell on the gun cupboard and for the first time in his fantasies about raiding the bank he thought of the actual money. He could spend it on anything he liked.

He could seek a mistress.

He thought about Angela Fiske, one of the girls in the bank. She was blonde and slim and pretty, and he liked watching her perch on her stool at the counter. She was the sort of girl he had dreamed of in his youth, when he had imagined women as needing protection. But other men had found the shy, gentle girls, and he had won a veritable Boadicea, one who was no longer an object of desire to him, and he doubted if anyone else found her desirable either, even when dressed in expensive clothes from stock. Briefly he remembered Isabel's solid flesh beneath him, the averted face, the rigid limbs, and his own desperate release. It was as well that no child had sprung from such unhappy couplings, but Robbie had experience of no other sort.

He had sometimes thought of finding a prostitute, but not in Harbington where he was known. He had telephoned Biddy, who offered massage, and had gone as far as her door when his courage failed and he fled. Other men talked about being given the come-on by women they met at parties, but Robbie went to few parties and if he was given the come-on he would not have realized what was happening.

It would soon be too late. He was forty-five, and the hair in front of his ears, which he had let grow long to be in the fashion, was turning white, though the rest of it was dark enough and still thick.

He rose and tried the door of the gun cupboard. It was locked, but he had already seen a bunch of keys in the drawer of Wilfred's desk. Robbie knew a little about guns; he had used an air rifle as a boy and there was his army training. Wilfred had a matched pair of twelve bore shotguns. Behind them in the cupboard was an odd one, and a fourth, with a shorter barrel. Then there were the two rifles.

Two minutes later the gun with the shorter barrel was in the boot of his 1100, together with six cartridges.

Robbie locked the cupboard and resumed his work. After a few minutes he took out his handkerchief and thoroughly wiped the key and the cupboard door, and the drawer of the desk. Wilfred would tell the police when he missed the gun.

But of course Robbie would return it unused, and soon. He was just testing his plan, to prove that it could be done.

Wilfred, returning, never noticed the missing gun. Robbie stayed to lunch, which was veal and ham pie and tomatoes, and then, when the rain eased off, helped Wilfred repair a fence in the afternoon. He took Wilfred out for dinner, just to the Star, which did excellent grills and had some good claret. Robbie wasted no time thinking of Isabel and her long day at the shop. She thrived on hard work, and the satisfaction she got from selling garments at more than double the price she bought them for, warded off all fatigue. She might expect to find him at home with dinner prepared as he usually was on Saturdays, but there was plenty of food in the freezer and she would not starve.

She was in bed when he got home.

He lit the gas fire and turned on the television set, just in time for the late night movie, a suspense thriller set in San Francisco.

The shotgun and the cartridges were still in the boot of his car.

Isabel stayed in bed for an extra hour on Sundays. Robbie took up her breakfast – coffee and toast, placing a folding tray-table, made by himself, across her knees.

Isabel sat up against soft pillows, her jet hair, dyed by Madge at The Scissor Box, standing up round her head in a fuzz. She poured out her coffee and carried the cup to her large, coarse lips, then gulped. Robbie, about to withdraw, stared at her with loathing. How had he once embraced that ugly body, now freed from its firm corseting? He saw the heavy, round breasts, pale below the red skin of the neck, a curious contrast, and thought about plunging a knife into the dark cleft between them.

'If you're planning to do some gardening today, don't waste your time here,' she said. 'There's plenty to do at the new house. No point in working here when we're leaving so soon.'

Robbie's broad beans were already through. Beneath cloches, early lettuce were hearting up. The new garden was an untidy pile of earth, unevenly spread, as the builders had left it.

'Get a gardening contractor if you want a garden made,' said Robbie shortly. 'I'm not going to do it.'

But he would, for how else would he spend his time?

He went downstairs and put out some crumbs for the birds. A fat thrush flew down to the table, and the robin who always perched near Robbie when he was digging. In time he could coax birds to come to the new house, he supposed.

Charlie came out when he saw the hose connected. He wore red rubber boots and stained corduroy trousers, his working garb. Robbie gave him a sponge and the boy followed him round, dabbing at mud on the Golf, which they tackled first.

'Mum says you've sold the house,' he said.

'Um – yes.' It could not be denied.

'So someone else'll be here.'

'Yes. But I'm not going far away,' said Robbie. 'To Windsor Crescent.'

'It's the other side of town. Mum said so,' said Charlie. 'I'll not be allowed to ride over there on my bike.'

'You will when you're older,' Robbie said. But when he was older, Charlie would have filled up his time with other activities. 'I'll miss you,' he said, then added more cheerfully, 'I'm not going yet.'

He never said 'we' unless it was unavoidable.

Charlie scrubbed industriously at a wheel. He was still too small to be much help, but he was a pleasant companion.

While they worked, the gun and the cartridges reposed in the boot.

Sometimes Isabel went out for lunch on Sundays; she visited Beryl Watson, her assistant. But today she was at home, and Robbie dished up the roast shoulder of lamb and new potatoes, with spring greens, which he had prepared, watching over the roast whilst attending to the cars. Isabel always carved. She slid the blade of the carving knife into the meat.

'I'm not moving,' Robbie told her.

'You'll have to. The contract is signed,' she replied, not looking up from her task. She had foreseen opposition from him, but not this obstinacy. He had never liked change, and he lacked all ambition. It was hard to remember, now, that once she had felt protective towards him, the only man she had been able to trap. Her tactic of keeping him out of bed until they were married had been the way to make sure of this inexperienced man. She had tried the other way and failed before she met Robbie, and she had enjoyed none of these encounters, but she had never expected to do so. Men's ways are nasty, her mother had told her, but marriage to one was the only guarantee of security, and the way to obtain social respect.

Things had changed now and independent women with careers abounded; nevertheless, it was as well not to have been passed over, and on the whole Robbie gave very little trouble. The present storm would pass.

'You can't make me go with you,' Robbie said.

'Where will you go, then? Into lodgings?' Isabel demanded. 'Oh no! We go our own ways. That suits me too. But we stay together. I'm having no scandal.'

Robbie rose from the table, ignoring his plate of succulent lamb, still pink as he liked it, and went out to his workshop. He sat down on the stool that faced his bench. In front of him, rows of tools hung on pegs, each in its own place, all shining. On the bench, an owl he had been carving from a piece of yew found on a walk across Wilfred's land, stared at him with blind eyes. He had his chance now to defy Isabel, to leave her and make some sort of life of his own.

But there would be a scandal; gossip. He knew that. In

this small town, where Isabel was well known and everyone recognized him as her husband, and at their age, there would be a great deal of talk and he would come off the worst, forfeiting sympathy. Even the bank would disapprove, although it could not dictate over that aspect of life. He could ask for a transfer away from the area but he would get no promotion. That would never come his way now.

But what if he sued for divorce? Isabel would object, but nowadays that was no obstacle, merely a question of time. He could begin again – find another wife, a young one, a warm and kindly one, there could even be children. . . . But here his thinking ran into a brick wall. There wouldn't be children.

He picked up the owl and the knife he used to shape it, and began cutting away at it, savagely, without any of his usual care and skill. Soon there was no owl left: just a heap of splinters and chippings.

In the house, Isabel finished her lunch; she stacked the dishes in the machine and put everything away, her only concession to his tantrum. He would work it off out there in his shed. He was too weak and idle to manage alone, and he had never, she was certain, looked at another woman since their marriage – or before it, come to that. He was inadequate in that department, but perhaps it did not stop him from the foolish thoughts other men of his age seemed to entertain and often to act upon. Beryl Watson's husband, for instance: at the age of forty-two he had left her for a young woman of twenty; so humiliating, though Beryl was much happier alone now that she had grown used to it. Isabel did not intend to suffer the same humiliation. Besides, Robbie was useful about the place.

When he realized that he had destroyed the owl he had spent so much time on, Robbie stormed out of the work-

25

shop, banging the door behind him and leaving the knife thrown down on the bench. He got into his car and backed noisily out into the road, crashing the gears as he changed into first. When he drove off he turned, from habit, towards Blewton.

Images raced through his mind. He remembered Isabel when they first met. She was trim in her uniform, though sturdy; not solid as she was now. Her body with its curves had been full of promise, but none had materialized. He knew that she had married him, not he her, and he still did not understand why; Robbie, accustomed now to women's emancipation, had forgotten older attitudes.

When he reached the familiar approaches to Blewton he slowed down, a little calmer now, and turned off at the crossing which led to the bank. He had never been there at a weekend before. He drove slowly along the quiet streets and stopped in the service road which ran past the row of shops that included the bank. A woman with a dog on a lead was walking by, but otherwise there was no one about. The shops had the blank, shuttered look common to Sundays, and the bank's heavy oak door looked very solid. He started the car up and drove round to the recreation ground. Here there was more activity: children played on the swings and the slide; dogs ran free. There were a number of young men about – fathers in charge of their children.

Robbie drove on into the main part of the town. He was not going home.

He thought about the gun in the boot of the car while he sat in the kindly darkness of a cinema watching a film called *The Killer*. When he reached home there was no one about to see him carry it into the house. He put it in the cupboard in his room, concealed behind his suits, and he put the six cartridges into one of his shoes.

3

Robbie's lunch habits varied. Most days, he brought sandwiches and ate them in the staff room, or, on fine days, in the recreation ground. He always went out for a stroll, and often shopped for the evening meal at the supermarket which was close to the bank. He carried a green Marks and Spencer carrier bag on these expeditions and sometimes he put it straight into the car before returning to the bank; at other times he brought it back with him. His dapper figure in the dark suit, or, in winter, the hip-length dark raincoat, carrying the bag, was a familiar sight to his colleagues. Most of them dashed quickly round the shops, too, in their lunch break.

Sometimes Robbie lunched at the Copper Kettle. This was a café two doors from the bank and it attempted, with oak tables and wheelback chairs, to wear an antique patina over its modern façade. When it opened, no one thought it would succeed, because the factories around had their own canteens and the customers for the shops were mostly local residents. But parking was easy in the streets close by and trade was being drawn to the neighbourhood from the centre of town; the café was prospering. It served tasty salads in pottery bowls; the portions were heaped into bowls too small, giving the appearance of generosity, but making it difficult to eat without scattering lettuce and tomato all over the table. Philip Grigson, the chief clerk, and Nigel West, the manager, both lunched there sometimes, though Nigel, who lived nearby, went home when his wife Susan was in, and Philip occasionally went to the Cross Keys on the corner for the steak and kidney pie for which the pub was renowned.

In his plan for robbing the bank, Robbie would eat sandwiches, for he would have to be quick. He would go to the recreation ground for his usual walk – so it would need to be a fine day. He could not devise an alibi since the shops would be closed, but his impeccable reputation would protect him.

On Monday he followed Angela Fiske round the supermarket. She bought yoghurt and an apple: her lunch. He debated inviting her to join him at the Copper Kettle, but he knew she would react with amazement. She might accept, but such an interlude could never lead to intimacy. Robbie was old enough to be her father, and she thought of him in the same category; he helped her sometimes when she got muddled about procedure; though Angela was now a cashier, she was a rather scatterbrained girl. How would she behave if faced with a gun held by a masked raider, Robbie wondered. He thought she might turn hysterical, which would be an excellent defence against a thief who meant to use no violence; she would forget to press her emergency alarm but her shrieks would alert the rest of the staff.

A successful raid must be carried out when a calmer cashier was on the till: Wendy Lomax, for example. She was older than the other girls and Robbie was surprised that she had stayed at the branch so long; there had been no vacancy there for promotion for some time but a capable girl like Wendy could have been offered a higher post at another branch. He had heard the other girls talking about her and some man called Terry, but Robbie did not know the full story; Terry and Wendy had gone

28

out together for several years and then Terry had, quite recently, dropped Wendy, he believed, but there must have been more to it than that. She had become rather quiet and withdrawn. She would not panic, faced with a gun. She was self-possessed enough to ring the alarm promptly so he would have to seem fierce to make her hand the money over instantly.

He went from the supermarket to a shop further along the street that sold stockings, and bought a pair.

'What size?' the girl wanted to know, and added, 'Are you sure you don't want tights?'

But Robbie wanted stockings, stretch ones, capable of great expansion. At home that night he pulled one on over his face. His features, compressed, stared back at him from the mirror, nose pale and eyebrows flattened: weird. He could have taken some of Isabel's old stockings from her drawer and they would not have been missed but he would touch nothing of hers that was personal. Long ago, he had bought stockings for her as gifts: not now. He had an arrangement with Gemma Gems in Harbington; before Isabel's birthday and before Christmas, she would go to the jeweller's shop and choose a charm for her loaded bracelet, or a different sort of bracelet – she wore several every day – earrings, or some other trinket. Robbie would then call to collect the item.

He could not walk from the lavatory in the recreation ground to pick up his getaway car wearing a stocking mask, and he could not stop in the car to put it on. Nor could he steal a car unmasked and recognizable.

He must find some other disguise.

Because his usual routine was disturbed, Wilfred Hunt did not miss his shotgun for some days. Normally on a Sunday he would have looked at his guns, might even have walked over his land with one, potting at rabbits or pigeon, but this Sunday he went over to Surrey to see his new grandson and was away all day. May was staying on for a little longer, so she did not perform her regular dusting ritual in the study, where the cowman's wife who came in to clean was allowed only to vacuum the floor.

Grateful for the order restored to his papers by Robbie, Wilfred deposited more on his desk as they arrived and hoped Jill, his secretary, would soon return.

He missed the gun on Wednesday.

At first he could not believe that it had gone. He checked the cupboard, which was properly locked, and the keys were in the drawer. Then he tried to remember when he had last seen it. He had not used a gun for over a fortnight, but it must have been there then or he would have noticed. The cowman might have borrowed it, though it was most unlikely.

'What, me? As if I would, Mr Hunt, without asking,' said Ben, when asked. 'And I don't know where you keep the keys to your cupboard, what's more.'

'No – well, I was sure you hadn't, Ben, but I had to ask you before I tell the police,' said Wilfred.

Ben thought of his son Barry, a good lad but one who had some dubious friends. Looking at his employer, he saw that the same thought was in his mind.

'I'll ask Barry, but I'm sure he never – ' Ben began.

Barry had an air rifle and often fired slugs at pigeons and sparrows; both men knew it. The farmer had warned the boy about the responsible use of firearms and thought that his words were heeded; all the same, Barry might have become ambitious.

'I won't get on to the police until you've spoken to Barry,' said Wilfred. Getting the lad into trouble for what might be just a prank could lead to serious consequences; if he had taken the gun – and Wilfred could see no other answer – it was better to deal with the matter amongst themselves.

He tucked the problem away at the back of his mind until Ben reported, the following day, that the boy denied all knowledge of the gun's whereabouts and that he, Ben, believed him. What was more, the boy's mother had searched his bedroom and the hut where he kept his motorbike, with no result. Barry was eighteen and worked for a builder; he had always seemed a dependable youth but now Wilfred was certain that he must have taken the gun and hidden it. He would question Barry himself, and toughly. Only if the boy continued to deny that he was the culprit would Wilfred tell the police.

So the gun's loss went unreported.

Isabel was choosing new curtains. She was absorbed by plans for the move to Windsor Crescent and all her thoughts that were not concerned with the business were directed towards it. Robbie came home to find patterns of fabric spread across chairs and pinned from the windows. She told him brusquely that she had selected a plain orange for his room: he was offered no choice.

On Thursday, at lunch time, he went into the public lavatory in the recreation ground. There was no one else in there, and he entered one of the cubicles. It was a damp day and his feet left prints as he crossed the floor. Shoes. He had not thought about them. Would a robber's shoes be seen in the bank? Not by a girl behind the counter, and the raid would not take place if there were any customers. However, unremarkable shoes must be worn.

He opened his briefcase and took out a folding nylon raincoat and an old tweed cap he had not worn for years. He put them into a polythene bag and reached up to push the bag behind the high, old-fashioned cistern. It was invisible from below. He took it out again, smiling. It was rather exciting. Sauntering out of the lavatory, he wandered across the recreation ground and then circled round its perimeter on the footpath. Cars were parked all along here, and he saw three with their keys in the ignition.

In his own personality he could mark down a likely car, then go to the lavatory and assume his disguise, which would include more than just the raincoat and cap, but he had not prepared the rest yet. Then, disguised, he would take the car, drive to the bank, in imagination conduct the raid, return the car and resume his normal appearance.

He thought of a simpler plan.

The disguise could be taken to the bank in the morning in a carrier bag inside his familiar Marks and Spencer carrier, and left in the staff room in his briefcase. At lunch time he could remove the two carriers – and a third, for the money. He must not be lumbered with his briefcase. After the raid he could put the money and the disguise in his car, leaving nothing in the lavatory at all. But unless the day was fine there would be his ordinary raincoat and hat to be hidden and they were too bulky to wedge behind the cistern. It was a fair weather only plan.

But he would never do any of it – not even the car part: it was just a diversion.

Thinking of all this occupied Robbie while Isabel planned her interior decorations.

On Saturday, after he had done the books for Caprice, he drove up to London, something he rarely did. He left the car near Wembley, taking a tube into the centre. There, he consulted the Yellow Pages and found a theatrical costumier. He went to the address, where he bought a bushy ginger beard and a matching wig. At a branch of Woolworth's he bought some dark glasses.

He already had suitable gloves, an old pair, worn soft and pliable; he kept them in the car.

In the evening he went to the cinema.

4

Robbie tried the wig and the beard on when he reached home. He looked extraordinary in them: a hirsute monster with surprised brown eyes under brows already flecked with grey. But the brows would be hidden by the dark glasses: he tried them on too, and then his old tweed cap. It needed a good pull to get it on over the wig.

He was totally unrecognizable: just a mass of brilliant hair with the cap and the glasses. He smiled at himself in the mirror as he slid his arms into the lightweight raincoat that was designed to take up little more space than a handkerchief. In it, he looked bulky. He pirouetted round his room, but quietly, for Isabel was asleep below.

Then he took out the gun. He tried loading and unloading it; it was quite easy, but now he saw how impractical it was to use a shotgun on such a raid. It was too large to conceal. He loaded it again and pointed it down at the floor. If he fired at Isabel, in bed below, would he hit her or would the cartridges bury themselves in the floor? What if he tried it? He could plead an accident – manslaughter. It would be worth serving a few years in prison to be free.

But he could be free of Isabel without so drastic a deed. He had only to walk out.

He put the gun away.

In the morning, as he walked along to Darcy's for the paper, his actions of the night before seemed farcical.

Reality was collecting the *Sunday Express* and the *Sunday Telegraph* and buying some toffees for Charlie. Then the short walk home as he studied the headlines: a strike threat; a murder in Soho; the arrest of a drug pusher.

He took Isabel up her tray, with the *Telegraph* neatly folded beside her napkin. The first time he had ever taken her breakfast in bed, he had put a single rose on the tray. She had roared with laughter and thrown it on the floor. On that occasion he had hoped to be admitted into bed again himself.

Over twenty years later he could stand back and marvel at his youthful naïvety. As a boy he had enjoyed reading tales of adventure in which heroines were rescued from dire fates; he saw himself as some sort of knight. True, Isabel wanted to be rescued from the NAAFI, but she needed no defending. Over the years she had told him often enough that he showed no initiative or drive. He had worked hard and conscientiously at the bank, but he lacked whatever quality was required for advancement. He seemed to need protection: the protection of the bank by day, and the domestic protection of Isabel's dominance.

Attempting to analyse his plight, Robbie was ashamed of his own weakness.

He opened Isabel's door and once again set the bed-table across her knees.

'You must sort out your shed,' she told him. 'You can't take it to Windsor Crescent. It wouldn't look well at all. It's much too shabby. Your bench can go in the garage.' She did not want to stop his carpentry; it was a useful hobby and it kept him out of the house when she wanted to be in it. 'Throw away all that rubbish you've got stacked there,' she added. 'Those old rags and tins of paint.'

Robbie did not answer her. He turned and left the room. When he had finished his own breakfast he went out to his workshop and picked up a block of wood. He began whittling it into the shape of a dagger, and had nearly finished it when Charlie came round to see if they were going to wash the cars, as usual. Robbie gave him the wooden dagger.

Wilfred Hunt was sure that Barry was telling the truth. He had known the boy for most of his life – had given him a lamb to keep as a pet when he was small and had taught him to drive the tractor when he was older. Now he faced Barry across his desk, like a headmaster, and repeated his question.

'You didn't come in here one day when I was out and borrow the gun, Barry?'

'No, Mr Hunt.'

'If you did, and you tell me and give it back, we'll forget the whole thing. No harm's been done,' said Wilfred.

'I didn't take it.' Barry's mouth set in a sulky line.

'It's a very dangerous weapon. If it got into the wrong hands – '

'I know that. I didn't take it,' Barry repeated.

Wilfred sat back.

'I believe you, Barry,' he said, and then, 'You hadn't mentioned to any of your friends that there are guns here?'

'No. But farmers always has guns,' said Barry.

'That's true. Well, I'm sorry, Barry – I'll have to report its loss to the police now and I expect they'll want to question you. I'll tell them I'm sure some outsider took it.'

Robbie took his disguise to work with him on Monday morning. He put the beard, the wig, the dark glasses, the cap and the raincoat into a plain white carrier bag and packed them in his briefcase. They spent the day there, at the bank, and he left them in the case when he went home on Monday night.

That evening there was a meeting of the Horticultural Society, and the chairman, who was one of Isabel's customers, inquired about the impending move.

'I do think you're wise,' she said. 'Those new houses are quite charming. But won't you miss your lovely garden? Have you taken lots of cuttings in preparation?'

'Not really,' said Robbie. 'I thought I'd beg slips from everyone here, and help too,' he added, in the joking tone he used at such times. But as he heard himself answer he knew he was compounding the facts: the Robinsons were moving and by implication it was with his consent; once again he had taken the line of least resistance.

'A much better neighbourhood for you,' nodded the chairman, who was the widow of a pharmacist. 'I'm surprised you didn't do it years ago – Claremont Terrace isn't what it was.'

Robbie said, 'I'll miss the neighbours.'

The chairman looked rather surprised at this remark and declared the meeting open.

Tuesday was wet. Robbie had brought no sandwiches today and he lunched at the Copper Kettle. He chose soup, a baked potato stuffed with sour cream, and cherry pie. While he ate, he did the crossword in the paper. At another table Angela Fiske and the bank's typist, who was new, were eating rolls and butter: an economical meal. Angela waved at Robbie cheerfully and the typist smiled bashfully as Robbie waved back.

Pulling his raincoat collar up, Robbie walked round to the recreation ground. He passed two cars with keys in their ignition. He went round the dripping laurels and into the lavatory. There was no one else there, and as he had done before, he entered a cubicle. Once inside, he opened his briefcase and took out the carrier containing, this time, his complete disguise. He stuffed it behind the cistern, pulled the chain and left.

He would leave it there overnight, as a test: but of what?

That evening Isabel was out. He did not know where she was, nor did he care, but guessed she had gone to have supper with Beryl Watson. Beryl lived in a remote hamlet six miles from the shop; there were several other cottages, transformed from farmworkers' cottages into pretty weekend hideouts for fugitives from town, but Beryl's was the only one that was occupied all the time; it had been a weekend retreat for her and her husband, and when they parted, in relief at gaining his freedom her husband had given her the cottage. Beryl found it rather isolated and Isabel often went there.

Alone in the house, Robbie roamed around it. He felt at home only in his own room and the kitchen: the sitting room was furnished to Isabel's taste with a gold-covered sofa and matching armchairs, and glass-topped occasional tables. He was always afraid of knocking something over or marking the upholstery. It had been far more comfortable before Isabel prospered and could buy all these things, when it was equipped with chairs they had bought at auctions, and tables he had made himself. Isabel had given all the old things to jumble sales.

He opened the door of her bedroom and looked in. There was a faint smell of furniture polish; the cleaning woman had been today. Isabel's dressing-table was quite bare; all her pots and unguents were kept hidden in drawers. She was very tidy. Her clothes all hung in the cupboard he had built for them. If he opened it, he would smell the bitter scent she used; or perhaps it was the scent of her own body. He closed the door.

The spare bedroom, with its twin beds under counterpanes of quilted nylon taffeta, was quite impersonal. It was seldom used. Isabel had a sister who came with her husband at increasingly rare intervals for brief visits; they lived in Liverpool. Robbie had no relatives of his own, and no old friends; he had kept up with none of his childhood acquaintances nor anyone he had met in the army.

He liked the kitchen in this house. He spent a lot of time in it, and he enjoyed its outlook over the garden. He knew what was expected of him here, and he had learned to avoid a lot of what he did not like. A whole new pattern would have to be devised at Windsor Crescent.

If he did not defy Isabel now, he never would: the rest of his life would be like the two decades past – meaningless. He walked slowly up the stairs to his own room, playing a game with himself: if he found the disguise still in position behind the cistern the next day, put it on, walked to the bank and entered, then left at once as if he had gone into the wrong building, and was able to resume his own identity without a hitch, he would leave Isabel. To make the test complete, he must also discover, though not steal, a car with a key in place. If it rained, the experiment was ruled out, because he would need to wear his own raincoat and hat out of doors and could not hide them while he wore the disguise.

He had no gun, so it was all just a charade.

He opened the drawer in his room where he kept trophies he had acquired through sending in cereal packet tops. There was a toy boat, a fire engine, a sheriff's badge. And there was a toy pistol, made of some sort of plastic that looked metallic, a dull grey in colour.

5

During the night the rain stopped, and in the morning the radio weather forecast prophesied sunny intervals during the day. Robbie cut two <u>rounds</u> of bread and buttered them; he filled the sandwiches with cheese and wrapped them carefully in a polythene bag which he put in his briefcase, with the newspaper and his Marks and Spencer carrier. He tucked another carrier, a blue one, inside the green Marks and Spencer bag, and in that was the toy pistol; the bag itself, however, was to hold the money.

The sky was still overcast when he reached Blewton and parked the car by the recreation ground, so he wore his raincoat and brown felt hat to the bank, but he took the old gloves out of the car and pushed them into his pocket.

The day began normally. The new typist was feeling less strange; Philip Grigson was feeling important because Nigel West, the manager, was away on a week's holiday in Majorca. The supervisor's varicose veins were aching and once again she thought about having them treated. Angela Fiske's head was full of her new boyfriend who was taking her out to a disco that night, and Wendy Lomax was still trying not to think about Terry, for whom she had turned down promotion. She had stayed in Blewton to be near him; when they met he was married, but soon afterwards he and his wife parted. His affair with Wendy had lasted for four years; then his wife had divorced him as she wanted to remarry and Wendy had expected, at last, to marry Terry. Instead, he had married someone else, a girl of twenty-two whom he had met at a party and of whose existence Wendy was unaware.

Wendy's immediate hurt had now turned to anger. She had given up so many years to Terry and she had let a good opening as first cashier at a different branch of the bank pass her by. Now she was thinking of transferring to another area where she could make a new start. Fresh surroundings might help her to forget about Terry, and there was no reason why she should not rise high in the bank; the married women cashiers tended not to want advancement, as their aim was to fill in two or three years while they built up their homes before starting families. Wendy had missed out. She would not marry now so she would make a life out of her career.

She had an early lunch hour and the shops were still open when she left the bank. She went to the chemist's, and to the cleaner's to collect a skirt, then into The Copper Kettle; since Terry's departure she had gone there a lot, for the therapy of eating well, and she had put on weight. The coffee gâteau which was one of their puddings was, Wendy had found, very hard to resist.

The newly dedicated career woman sat down to a lunch of chicken risotto and coffee cake, with a Jean Plaidy novel from the library. She felt better when she returned to the bank, and to her solitary place at the counter.

When one o'clock came along, Robbie wondered about the weather and asked Wendy, returning, if it was fine.

'The sun's out,' she said.

So Robbie left his raincoat and hat in the bank but he took his gloves out with him, tucked into the Marks and Spencer green carrier which also held the pistol in the spare carrier, and his sandwiches.

There were a few cars parked near his own. Suppose he

used his own and then alleged it had been stolen? That should complicate things – but then he would have to abandon it some distance from the bank, which would run him short on time. The notion amused him, however, as he ate his sandwiches on a bench in the recreation ground, under a thin, fitful sun. When he had finished them, he sauntered across and looked at the cars. None had a key within. So he couldn't do it – take one and park it outside the bank. He went into the lavatory, which again was deserted, and into the cubicle where he had left his disguise. It was still there, in the carrier behind the cistern.

He could put it on, walk into the bank and act as if he'd forgotten something, so that he could leave immediately, resume his normal appearance and return to duty in plenty of time before his lunch hour ended. That was enough of a challenge. Robbie stood in the small cubicle which smelled of urine and disinfectant and put on the wig, the beard, the dark glasses, the raincoat and the cap. He put on the shabby gloves, and he put the empty carrier which had held the disguise inside the green one, stuffing them both behind the cistern to wait for his return from what was to be really just a dress rehearsal. Finally he put the toy pistol in his pocket.

Then he came out of the lavatory, carrying the empty blue bag, and walked towards the bank, after several strides adjusting his normal brisk pace to a more loping tread.

He met no one, and the service road by the bank was empty except for a red Renault parked outside the Copper Kettle, almost opposite the bank. He swerved and glanced inside it. The keys were in the ignition.

So he could have carried out the whole raid today. The weather was right; there was no one about; he had a car; all that now remained was for the bank to be free of customers.

He opened the door and it was. Wendy Lomax, the only cashier on duty, was sorting out dirty and torn notes, her till open.

Suddenly Robbie was standing in front of her, the gun in his hand, pointing it at her beneath the glass.

'Keep quiet. Give me the money,' he growled hoarsely. 'All the notes.'

Wendy, seeing the shadow of a customer at the counter, had been on the point of putting down what she was doing to attend to him, when she heard the gruff voice and saw the dull grey snout of a gun pointing at her. She was aware of the brown-gloved hand, the knuckles stained with oil.

The bank's instructions were not to have a go. As she pressed the alarm she began, very slowly, to take out the money.

'Hurry up,' snarled the voice.

Wendy took as long as she could. Delay was inevitable before the alarm could be relayed from the security system to the police, but surely someone would look over from the rear of the bank and see what was happening? The robber had picked his time well, though; most of the staff were still at lunch and he would be screened from anyone who did look across at them by her body. He would seem just an ordinary customer. She pushed the wads of notes over the counter and saw the gloved hand with the gun begin scooping them into an open carrier bag held in the raider's other hand. He thrust the money into the carrier very quickly, and while he did it the gun still pointed at her. Wendy thought, I must be able to describe him, and she looked up from the counter and the threatening hand to his face. She saw a tweed cap and a mass of red, untidy hair, some on the raider's head and some forming his beard; she saw the dark glasses. Then the man was gone. Only seconds had passed.

Robbie's heart thudded as he ran out of the bank and across to the car. He pulled open the door and flung himself inside, throwing the laden carrier on to the seat beside him. The controls were unfamiliar to him and he was rough with the clutch as he moved off, but afterwards he thought it was because the dark glasses obscured his vision that he failed to see the woman who seemed to spring up from the ground in front of the car. He pulled the steering wheel round but he struck her. There was a loud thump and she vanished.

Robbie drove on, round the corner towards the recreation ground, past his own car towards the laurel hedge that screened the lavatory. He went inside and took off his disguise. Then he pulled the carriers from behind the cistern and put it all – the dark glasses, the wig, the beard, the cap and the raincoat – back into the white carrier. The gun went in with them, and the carriers, the blue one which held the money, and the white one, he loaded into the large green Marks and Spencer bag. Then, wearing the gloves, he left the lavatory and walked over to his own car where he calmly opened the boot and dropped the green carrier inside. Then he opened the driver's door and got in. He sat there for a little while with his heart thumping, unable to believe what he had actually done.

I must get back to the bank, he thought. I mustn't be late.

He took off the gloves and put them in the locker where they normally lived. Then he got out of the car and locked it. He told himself that he had been moving so slowly that the woman could barely have been brushed by the car, but the thump as it hit her had been considerable. As he turned the corner to walk towards the bank he saw two police cars already drawn up, and there was a huddle of people bending over something that lay by the kerb.

Robbie walked faster when he got near to the bank. The normal reaction of a trusted employee when he saw that something was wrong was to discover what it was, and when a constable at the door told him he could not enter, Robbie protested.

'What's the trouble, constable?' he asked, with the command that would have earned him promotion had he only shown it years before. 'I am the first securities clerk here. I've been at lunch.'

'Oh, thank goodness you're back, Robbie,' came a voice from behind the officer. It was Philip Grigson, on whom the mantle of greatness was now lying like a mighty burden. 'Please let Mr Robinson in,' he added to the policeman.

'I can see there's been an accident,' Robbie said, gesturing towards the scene in the road, where the supervisor and Angela Fiske were among the people gathered around the body that lay on the ground. He had not expected that, thinking an ambulance would have arrived long since, but it had to come from right across town, through the dense traffic in the centre. Even with bell and blue light that would take time.

'There's been a raid on the bank, sir,' the policeman was saying. 'The getaway car hit a woman.'

Robbie wanted to ask if she was badly hurt, who she was, all sorts of things, but he did not: as a bank employee his immediate concern should be for the safety of the staff and the security of the money.

'Is anyone hurt in here?' he asked, stepping inside.

He saw that the staff remaining in the building were clustered together in the rear working area behind the counter, obviously shocked. A constable was with them. The door to the manager's office was open and Wendy

44

Lomax was seated on a chair by the desk; there was another policeman with her. Philip Grigson almost fell on him with relief.

'Robbie, we've been held up,' he said.

The policeman who was in the office with Wendy emerged. To his eye, the newcomer appeared senior to Philip Grigson but he already knew that the young man was acting manager in the manager's absence.

'This is Mr Robinson,' Philip said distractedly.

'You've been to lunch, I gather, Mr Robinson,' said the second policeman. 'Did you see anything? Which way did you come?'

'From the recreation ground. I always go there at lunch time, if it's fine. For a stroll,' said Robbie.

'Did you see a red Renault? I rushed out in time to see it vanish round the corner,' said Philip.

'No, I didn't notice one,' said Robbie. 'How long ago did this happen?' He glanced at the clock on the wall. He was back a few minutes early, as usual.

'Fifteen minutes. Wendy looked at the clock right away,' said Philip.

'Sensible girl.' approved Robbie. 'Well done.'

He felt as if he were acting in a play. None of this was taking place in real life and it was easy to act as if he did not know what had happened. Some other person seemed to have invaded his body for the past three-quarters of an hour and taken independent action, and he was responsible for none of it.

'He'll be miles away by now,' said the policeman.

While they were talking, the ambulance, bell clanging, arrived outside. Angela Fiske and Betty Fox, the supervisor, returned to the bank a few minutes later, and Angela was white faced.

'There was blood all over the place,' she said, turning even paler, and she had to be put into a chair with her head thrust forward to prevent her from fainting. Wendy Lomax, however, victim of the hold-up, appeared calm, talking to the policeman who had now returned to her and who had his notebook out.

While all this was happening another car arrived outside and two more men came into the bank: they were policemen, but they were in plain clothes.

'My name's Thomas,' said one of them, a thin man, dark, with a pale, lined face. 'Detective Inspector Thomas, and this is Detective Sergeant Briscoe.' He spoke to Robbie. 'Are you the manager?'

'No. Mr West is away,' said Robbie, and motioned Philip Grigson forward. 'This is Mr Grigson, who is acting in his place.'

Philip had pulled himself together. He could not be blamed for the raid having happened.

'They didn't get away with much,' he said. 'About three thousand pounds in notes.'

'They – were there two of them? More than two?' pounced Thomas.

'Only one came into the bank,' said Philip. 'But he may have had someone outside in the car. I couldn't tell as it drove away.'

'What about the car?' Thomas snapped, and a constable told him about the Renault. Thomas nodded and said, 'It's too late for road blocks. Where's the young lady who saw the robber?' He looked at Angela, now reviving.

'Miss Lomax is in the office,' said Philip, and pointed. Thank goodness he'd been in the bank himself, not out at lunch but eating sandwiches. It would sound good to head office.

'Right.' Thomas gave a nod to his sergeant and the two men vanished into the office, closing the door behind them.

Philip Grigson looked appealingly at Robbie.

'Better advise head office,' he suggested, and Philip, glad of some action, went off to do it.

The rest of the staff were talking to one another, but in a moment Detective Sergeant Briscoe came out of the manager's office and spoke to one of the other policemen who began to shepherd them together, ready to take their statements. There were customers outside, now, who were being turned away. One of the policemen took Robbie off to a desk and asked him to describe what he had seen. Robbie repeated his account of his return to the bank. Before that, he said, he had eaten his sandwiches in the recreation ground and then gone for a walk around, as it was fine; his usual custom.

In the manager's office, Detective Inspector Thomas was thinking with some relief that Wendy Lomax looked calm and sensible.

'Did you get much of a look at him, Miss Lomax?' he asked.

'I don't know – I tried to think about doing that, but it was all so quick,' said Wendy. 'I think he must have been wearing a false beard. It was so bushy. And he had long red hair. It could have been a wig. He was extraordinary-looking. He had a tweed cap on – brownish. And dark glasses. And he was wearing a nylon raincoat – one of those thin ones that pack up small. Black.'

Briscoe was noting down what she said.

'I'd like you to come to the police station, Miss Lomax,' said Thomas. 'We'll see if you can help us to make up a photofit picture.'

'Now?' asked Wendy.

'Yes – in just a few minutes, if you'd be ready,' said Thomas, and turned to Briscoe. 'Get some more help down here sharp,' he instructed. 'I expect chummy wore gloves but we'd better see what we can pick up.'

'He did,' said Wendy, on her way towards the door to

47

fetch her coat. 'Brown leather ones, with a stain of some sort on one hand. The right hand, the one that was holding the gun.'

'We'll show you some pictures of guns, too, in case you can recognize what sort it was,' said Thomas. They'd got one or two actual weapons, which they could show her for real, too.

Wendy went off in a police car, and two detective constables arrived shortly after, to begin dusting around for fingerprints. Robbie knew that gloves could leave traces from which they could be identified and he knew that he must destroy his gloves, as a final protection for himself. But he felt very confident that no one would ever suspect the raider's true identity.

'Robbie, wasn't Wendy brave?' said Angela. 'I'm sure I'd have screamed immediately.'

'Then you'd probably have got shot,' said Philip Grigson.

'If you'd come back from lunch a bit sooner you might have caught him running away, Robbie,' Angela continued. 'Would you have had a go at him?'

'I hope so,' said Robbie. 'But how can one tell?'

'Head office want us to call back,' said Philip to Robbie. 'They'll probably send someone round tomorrow. The amount's not so large, and no one was hurt, and with the police here there's really nothing that anyone can do.'

'I suppose not,' Robbie agreed. 'Will they let us reopen?'

Philip went to inquire, and learned that the police would probably have finished their dusting for prints quite quickly. The bank could certainly open for a short time before its official closing hour.

'Business as usual,' said Philip, managing a smile. 'Well, there's work to do, everyone. Let's get on with it, except for those whom the police want to talk to, of course.'

Remarkably soon, normality returned. Robbie went to his desk and picked up his own work but he kept thinking of the woman who had been knocked down. If it hadn't been for that, the whole thing could soon have been forgotten, but he had started some sort of nightmare and because of her it would go on. He could not understand what had come over him in those seconds when he walked into the bank and saw Wendy, intent at her till, unaware that he had come in. By his wild action he had turned himself into an armed robber who would be hunted down with all the resources of the local constabulary.

The car would soon be found. But the police might not think of looking for it so near at hand, at first. Its owner would report it missing, of course – might already have done so. He felt unutterably weary, aware in his mind of all that he had done but quite unable to feel that the raid had had anything to do with him.

Betty Fox, the supervisor, thought everyone had had a shock. She set the typist on to making cups of tea for all, including the police, and opened a packet of ginger biscuits from her private store.

6

A police car brought Wendy back to the bank at half past four. Philip Grigson told her she should go home but she said no, she might as well get on with her work, she'd missed enough of it as it was.

Philip was eager to leave at the end of the working day. He had a date to meet Dawn Smyth that evening. He was keen to become engaged to Dawn, the daughter of the town clerk; he had marked her out as a very suitable mate for an ambitious man, which he was, and he had already made sure of her. It was now important to impress her parents, and Philip had mapped out his evening thoroughly. He was collecting Dawn from her home, and it had been arranged that he would arrive in good time, to be offered some sherry by her mother, on whom he would turn his charm. Dawn's father was at a meeting tonight and would be late. The idea was to earn the support of the mother before tackling the father, who was very possessive. Philip resolved to give a modest account of how well he had dealt with the aftermath of the robbery. Mrs Smyth would feel Dawn secure with so resourceful a young man.

'And then I rang up head office,' Philip would say.

All the same, he was still glad that Robbie had been there, and as they prepared to leave he suggested that Robbie might take Wendy home.

'She seems all right but she must be rather shaken. I know I am,' Philip admitted.

'Well – yes. You don't think one of the women – ?' Robbie tried, but did not persist. Betty Fox always hurried away, back to her invalid husband, and none of the other women had cars.

Wendy was very grateful for the offer of a lift. She didn't feel shaky, but it was nice to be sitting in Robbie's car instead of waiting for the bus. She lived about three miles from the bank across town. The journey was taken up with giving Robbie directions about the route and when they arrived outside the terraced house where she lived, she asked him if he would like to come in for a few minutes.

'To tell you the truth, Robbie, I don't feel like being left alone, right away,' she admitted.

She had always liked Robbie. He was quiet and kindly, almost cosy, and, unaware of Philip's intervention, she thought it typical of him to offer her a lift.

Since Robbie was responsible for Wendy's disturbance, he could not refuse. He followed her up the stairs to where she lived on the top floor and stood on the landing while she felt for her key in her handbag.

She lived in a large attic room, with a curtained recess at one end containing a sink and small stove. There was a gas fire, which Wendy immediately lit.

'Come in and sit down,' she said.

There was a divan bed in one corner, covered with a Welsh wool spread in various shades of red and purple, and two armchairs, a wing one upholstered in deep red velvet and a small tub chair in a linen cover. Wendy gestured Robbie towards the wing armchair. It was extremely comfortable and he said so.

'Yes, I know,' Wendy said, laughing. 'I bought it for five pounds about ten years ago and went to upholstery classes to learn how to do it up. It turned out all right.'

There were some prints on the white-painted walls – Van Gogh's 'Sunflowers' and two Canalettos. A vase of daffodils stood on the mantelpiece. The carpet was a drab, worn beige but there was a large sheepskin-type rug in front of the fire. On top of a bookcase there were some photographs, among them a handsome young man in naval uniform.

Wendy saw Robbie glance at it.

'That's my father,' she said. 'He was killed in the war just before I was born. My mother married again seven years ago – she and her husband live in Scotland. I go up there to stay for part of my holidays most years.' Except when I've been away with Terry, she thought. They had been to Corfu, to Yugoslavia and to Spain together. 'I stayed down here when my mother got married,' she added. 'I lived at home before that.' But then she had met Terry and their affair had begun. 'That was before you came – you were in the Harbington branch before you came to us, weren't you?'

'Yes.'

'Your wife runs that very good dress shop, doesn't she? Caprice?' Wendy asked. 'She has lovely things.'

'So they should be, at the prices she charges,' said Robbie, who was always shocked at the immense mark-up which Isabel put on her wares.

'I bought a dress there once,' said Wendy. 'It was expensive.' She bethought herself suddenly of her hostess duties and added, 'I've got some sherry. Would you like some, Robbie? Maybe it would do us good after all the shocks of the day.'

'It would be very nice,' said Robbie.

He watched her cross the room to a large, old-fashioned sideboard and begin pulling bottles out. Her green jersey dress was drawn tight round her sturdy body as she bent to open the door. Isabel had been much that shape at the same age, Robbie reflected; but her sturdiness had turned solid and unyielding.

'There, I knew there was some,' cried Wendy triumph-antly, plucking a bottle of Cyprus sherry from the back of the cupboard. She had arranged tins of spaghetti, soup and cereal packets on the floor in order to get at it. This was obviously her store cupboard.

Sipping his sherry, Robbie looked round the room in a more relaxed way.

'Do you cook in here?' he asked.

'There's a minute stove and a sink behind there.' Wendy pointed to the curtained recess. 'I use the bath-room on the floor below.'

'I like it,' Robbie said, and tried to decide wherein lay its charm. None of the contents would have been tolerated by Isabel except possibly the reproduction paintings. 'It's cosy,' he pronounced.

'I think so too,' said Wendy. 'I'd rather be here on my own than sharing a big flat.'

'How did you get on at the police station?' Robbie asked. It was a perfectly natural question under the circumstances.

'Oh – it was quite interesting, in rather a grim sort of way,' said Wendy. 'They were really very patient. I kept changing my mind about the photofit picture. I didn't register anything much about the man except his beard and hair. It must all have been a disguise. I couldn't describe his mouth or anything helpful, and his chin was all hidden. Still, they're going to circulate the result of our efforts. I don't think the inspector feels it will be much help.' She rose, and topped up Robbie's glass. 'We looked at guns, too – pictures of them, and a few real ones they've got. That was no help. It just looked like a small grey pistol to me – sort of pewter-coloured. I thought the in-spector was a bit disappointed I couldn't be more definite.'

'What about the woman who was run over?' Robbie asked. 'Is she badly hurt?'

'I haven't the slightest idea,' said Wendy. 'They didn't mention her while I was at the station.'

'I suppose she went to Blewton hospital?'

'Where else?'

Soon afterwards, Robbie left, but with some reluctance. For a moment he thought about inviting Wendy out for a meal. She seemed to have only tins in her larder. It had been very pleasant, sitting there chatting; despite everything, his tension had eased. But he had things to do. He must ring up the hospital to find out how the woman was who had been hurt in his escapade, and there was all that money in the car to be hidden away.

'Who was the woman who was hurt?' he asked, he hoped in a casual voice. 'Do you know that?'

'Yes. I did hear them mention it at the police station,' Wendy said. They had given her tea in a big china cup, with a digestive biscuit, while the inspector conferred with a colleague, and she had heard two constables talking. 'Her name's Helen Jordan. She doesn't come from Blewton – Wimbledon, I think they said.'

Wendy thought about Robbie as she opened a tin of spaghetti for her supper. He had seemed quite happy to stay indefinitely. If she hadn't known that he had a wife to return to, she might have asked him to stay for supper, although she had only tins and some eggs. She thought he would have been quite happy eating a scratch meal. She had lapsed into eating too many scratch meals herself lately; she filled up with bread and had developed a habit of watching the clock until it was time for the morning coffee break, at which she now often ate a chelsea bun coated in sugar which she bought on her way to work. She had put on pounds since Terry was married.

Robbie was probably going home to an exotic meal

cooked by his wife. Wendy remembered her visit to Caprice quite clearly. She was going up to London for a weekend with Terry and she had decided to buy a new dress, for once sparing no expense, since he was taking her to meet some business colleagues and she wanted to create a good impression. Caprice had the reputation for being a better dress shop than anything that could be found in Blewton, where there were various stores of the sort to be found in most large towns but few specialist shops. Caprice catered for the wives of the well-off business and professional men who lived in the area, many of whom commuted some distance to work.

She had looked first at the window, where there was a display in emerald green – two dresses, a skirt and a silk shirt, with a few accessories draped round them. It was a striking well-arranged display, and the clothes were elegant.

Wendy entered the shop, which was long and narrow, with two changing cubicles at the rear. Garments hung in racks along the walls, and there was a section of shelves containing shirts and sweaters. A young woman came forward to serve Wendy, who said she was looking for a light wool dress for a lunch party – pink.

Miriam, Isabel's chief assistant, showed her various dresses and Wendy hummed and ha'd and changed her mind about colour. Another customer came in, and Wendy asked to be left to look through the clothes on her own while the assistant took care of her. Then the telephone rang, and a woman came through from the rear of the shop. She gave the impression of being tall, but in fact she was not much taller than Wendy. She was squarely built, smartly dressed in a green and navy two-piece, and she had stiffly set jet-black hair, sprayed with lacquer. She was well made up and looked rather like a successful headmistress. She came straight over to Wendy after she had concluded a short, sharp conversation on the telephone, and in no time at all Wendy was sure she had been summed up as not wealthy enough to shop here.

'I want a pink dress,' she repeated. 'I've looked at several. Your – er – your colleague showed me some, but none of them is quite right.'

'You'd look better in green, or even blue,' said Isabel. 'Pink isn't easy after a certain age.'

Thank you, thought Wendy, but the way in which it was said somehow robbed the words of offence.

'Now, cyclamen,' Isabel was saying. 'We've got something outside that's just come in – I'll fetch it.'

She disappeared, and returned in a few minutes carrying a dress in a deep bluish pink which she held against her own body so that Wendy could see it properly. 'This colour would suit you,' she said. 'It would do things for you. Why not try it on?'

Wendy was soon in a cubicle, doing just that, and it was true: the colour was perfect for her, and it was her exact size. She looked at the price tag. Even that was not extortionate. Robbie's wife had picked out a possible purchase for her, coaxed her to try it on, and left the rest to the dress. She certainly knew her job, and she had been pleasant and easy although she looked rather formidable.

Wendy bought the dress and it was a success.

That efficient woman, with the rigid hair and the corseted body, for Wendy had realized she was moulded behind powerful elastic, was the one that Robbie went home to each night. It was difficult to picture them together.

She had just finished her meal and was washing up when she had a caller. The wild, irrational hope that it might be Terry surged up, to be sent away sternly: habit died hard.

It was Detective Inspector Thomas. He was alone.

56

'Miss Lomax – I'm sorry to trouble you again, but if I might have a word – ' he said, on the landing.

Wendy unlatched the chain and opened the door.

'Of course. Come in,' she said.

'Glad to see you've got that chain,' said Thomas. 'It's not very secure here, is it? Anyone can walk in.'

'That's true,' said Wendy. The front door of the house was often left on the latch, although all the tenants had a key. 'But I don't think anyone who lives here is worth robbing.'

'Everyone's got a pound or two lying about, or items worth a few quid,' said Thomas.

'Yes – well – ' Wendy knew he had not come to lecture her on security. 'Sit down, won't you?'

Thomas sat down in the velvet armchair and Wendy faced him in the small tub chair.

'The raid this afternoon,' Thomas began.

'Yes?'

'You're our best – really our only witness.'

'I know. I've told you everything I can think of,' said Wendy.

'You've been very helpful,' said Thomas. 'But I just thought that away from the station, and now you've had time to get over the shock a bit, something else might have come to mind.'

'What sort of thing?'

'Well – the voice, for instance. You said it was a sort of snarl.'

'Yes. Maybe I'd know it again if I heard it.'

'It wasn't foreign? Or like a dialect?'

'He only said, "Give me the money",' said Wendy. 'And then "Hurry". You couldn't really tell. It didn't sound foreign.'

'We've found the car he used,' said Thomas. 'The red Renault that knocked down Mrs Jordan.'

'Oh – well, that's good. Isn't that a start?' said Wendy. 'Where was it?'

'Not far away. Just round the corner in Johnson Road, near the recreation ground.'

'How did you know it was the same car?'

'We checked it out – checked the number. It belongs to a James Jordan – Mrs Jordan's husband.'

'What? So she was knocked down by her own car?'

'Yes. She must have seen the thief driving off in it and tried to stop him. Probably realized she'd left the keys in it – very careless, that.'

'Do you think he drove at her deliberately?' asked Wendy.

'It looks a bit like it,' said Thomas.

'I wonder why he left it so near? You'd think he'd hurry off as far as he could, after that,' said Wendy.

'Yes, you would – but he'd know we'd be after the car. He may not have been certain that no one had the number. He may be a very cool customer who walked away from the Renault, perhaps without his disguise, and picked up another car quite quickly. We're checking reports of stolen cars but nothing definite's turned up yet. There are several cars missing in Blewton, I'm afraid. With a town this size it keeps happening, and the owners ask for it half the time.'

'By leaving their keys in?'

'Exactly,' said Thomas, and smiled.

He seemed to be settling down for a considerable stay. Wendy wondered if she should offer him the rest of the sherry.

'Where's the sergeant?' she asked.

'At the hospital. Mrs Jordan's come round and he's trying to talk his way past the doctors to see her.'

'Poor thing – I hope she'll be all right,' said Wendy. 'Has her husband come?'

'We haven't been able to get hold of him. Someone's been to their home address but there's no one there. It seems Mr Jordan often goes abroad on business so he may be away.'

'Can't you find out?'

'Oh, yes. We'll get on to him through his firm,' said Thomas, who knew that his colleagues in the Metropolitan Police were doing just that. 'But it may take a bit of time to bring him back from wherever he's gone to.'

'Oh dear,' said Wendy. 'I wonder what she was doing down here.'

'She works in a photographic studio near her home, it seems,' said Thomas. 'Maybe she was down here on a job. They may do industrial photography. But you'd expect local firms to employ local photographers. Still, we'll soon know about that. Was he left-handed?'

He shot the question at Wendy.

'No,' she said at once. 'I told you – he held the gun in his right hand and scooped the money with it into a carrier bag that he held in his left. A blue bag. I don't think there was any writing on it – it may have been a plain one.'

She had been sure when they talked before, and she was sure now. If the police traced this villain, she would be a very safe witness to the extent of what she had seen. Thomas was less concerned about the three thousand pounds the bank had lost than the accident to Mrs Jordan, but the amount of the robbery did not lessen the degree of evil employed: Wendy Lomax had been held up at gun point.

'If it hadn't been for our protective glass barrier, I might have managed to throw something at him,' said Wendy.

'It's a very good thing you didn't. He might have shot you,' said Thomas.

59

Wendy smiled.

'Well – it's easy to sound brave now it's all over,' she said. 'I don't suppose I'd really have done anything like that. The woman couldn't have been his accomplice, could she? She might have been hurrying back to the car to join him.'

'A fine way to treat her, if so,' said Thomas.

'No – I suppose that isn't a good idea,' said Wendy. 'But she must have followed him pretty quickly when he took the car, to have caught up with him.'

'She didn't have to. She was having lunch in The Copper Kettle. One of the waitresses told us that. She must have left the car outside while she was eating. We'll be able to establish that – someone will have seen it.'

'So the thief took the car on the spur of the moment?'

'Yes.'

'That supports your theory that he was a pretty cool customer who meant to walk away,' she said.

'He may have had his intended getaway car waiting round the corner,' said Thomas. 'Then used the Renault when he saw it handy.'

'Doesn't sound like a very well-laid scheme to me, if he changed it at the last minute like that,' said Wendy.

'I think it may have been very well laid,' said Thomas. 'Then he improvised, and hit that woman.'

'If she dies – ' said Wendy.

'Exactly.' Thomas's voice was grim.

'Well, I'm sorry I couldn't describe him properly for you,' Wendy said again.

'You didn't really notice his mouth, did you?' Thomas said. 'You had trouble with that, with the photofit.'

'I had trouble with the whole thing,' said Wendy. 'All I really saw was a lot of hair and some dark glasses. Usually with beards you do notice lips – rather odd they seem, pink among all that hair. But I don't think his showed.'

'You don't like beards,' said Thomas.

'I haven't a lot of experience of them,' said Wendy. 'Shall I make some coffee?'

'That would be nice,' said Thomas. 'Thanks.'

He should leave really. He had known all along that she was unlikely to be able to add to her statement. They were getting nowhere. But he watched her put on the kettle and thought that perhaps they were, in a way.

On his way home after leaving Wendy, Robbie stopped at a telephone box to inquire about Mrs Jordan. At first he thought of saying he was inquiring on behalf of the bank, but then he wondered if this might lead to problems: suppose Philip Grigson, or someone from head office, had already done that?

He adopted the deep, gruff voice he had used in the raid and made his inquiry, to learn that her condition was unchanged.

This told him nothing, but he dared not press it. More would be known the next day and he would inquire again. There was nothing to do now but drive home. Back to Isabel.

He heard her in the kitchen when he arrived. He went straight up to his room with his briefcase and the green Marks and Spencer carrier bag which contained all the evidence of his crime, including the money, and he locked it all in his cupboard.

Isabel was having dinner in the dining room when he came downstairs, leaving the kitchen for him; they rarely ate together. He opened the door and went in. She was sitting at one end of the mahogany table, a glass of red wine at her side and a large, succulent steak from which the raw juices poured on a plate before her. The wine bottle, half full, was on the sideboard. Her face was flushed. She would finish the bottle this evening.

She looked up in surprise at the intrusion of her husband.

'The bank was raided today,' said Robbie, and before she could comment he went on. 'There was only one robber. He didn't get away with much – about three thousand pounds. No one was hurt in the bank but he hit some passer-by as he drove off afterwards.'

'Brute,' said Isabel.

What would you think, wondered Robbie, if you knew the brute was standing beside you, was married to you?

'Yes,' he said, and added, 'He was armed.'

'So you didn't have a go at him,' Isabel sneered.

'I was out at lunch,' snapped Robbie. 'I came back to find the police at the bank.'

Suppose he went upstairs to his room and donned his disguise, picked up the pistol and threatened Isabel: how would she react then? Would she see through it and tell him not to be childish?

He did not put it to the test.

'I thought you'd better be told,' he said, and closed the door upon her and her repast.

In the kitchen he felt like having some more sherry, but the decanter was in the dining room and so were the reserve bottles. However, there was some cooking sherry in the larder and he poured himself out a large glass of that. After drinking it, he opened a tin of duck soup and cut himself a thick slice of bread. This was his meal. Then he went out to his workshop and looked at his stock of wood. He took out a pencil and pad and made a neat sketch, writing measurements down.

Wendy Lomax had no coffee table. He had made several in the past, which he had sold. He'd make her one.

He might not actually find the courage to give it to her, but he'd make it with her in mind. He'd got some elm, which might be good for the top. Or why not make it of oak? He spent some time working on various designs and amending them, before deciding on the final pattern.

After Isabel had gone to bed he went into the sitting room and turned on the television but he had missed the news so he did not know if the Blewton bank raid was important enough to feature on the national networks. There was a discussion about battered wives in progress on one channel, and on another there was a film about a pop musician.

Robbie switched off the set and sat in the silent room. He looked at the gold striped paper; the reproduction furniture placed just so on the Wilton carpet; the electric fire with its false coal glow in the hearth. It was like something out of a magazine, and the sitting room in the new house would be an advance upon it. Then he thought of Wendy's small, rather cluttered room, and of Wendy herself, with her ordinary face, scarcely made up, the dark blue eyes which had looked at him across the counter as he pointed the gun at her, showing fear that was instantly suppressed. Those same eyes had looked at him with an easy, frank gaze as he sipped sherry by her gas fire. He had always thought her a pleasant girl.

He wished that he was with her now, and he wished that the clock might be put back so that none of the afternoon's events had happened.

He still couldn't understand how they had.

7

On Thursday morning the raid was reported in some of the daily papers; more prominence was given to the hit and run accident than to the actual robbery, and there were poignant words about the absence overseas of Mrs Jordan's husband. He had, however, been traced, and was on his way home. Wendy, as the threatened cashier, was not mentioned by name. Detective Inspector Thomas had said they would try to hide her identity, though probably someone would discover it in the end.

Wendy had slept dreamlessly: the sherry, perhaps, she had thought as she ate her Weetabix. She arrived at the bank just after Robbie; he asked her at once if she had felt any ill effects from the day before.

'None,' she said cheerfully.

Robbie wondered what she would say if he asked her out one evening. There was a new *trattoria* in Bury Street that was supposed to be good: chianti and candlelight. He was so much older than she that he thought she might look upon him in a different way than a man nearer her age, and the fact of his being married might not matter.

He played with the idea during the day. It was better than thinking about the injured woman. He had telephoned the hospital on the way to work and the words of the night before had been repeated: condition unchanged, but a restful night. There was little solace in that.

The robbery was the topic of the day among the staff. Had it been a long-planned job? What if the bank had been busy at the time – would the robber have used his gun? Would the police catch the thief? Betty Fox reported that her husband thought they would not try very hard as the amount stolen was, by some standards, not large, and no one was hurt.

'They were. That woman, Mrs Jordan – she was hurt,' said Wendy. 'And I'm sure the police will try very hard to catch the robber.' She was certain of this, after Thomas's visit the night before. But she did not mention that he had been round to see her.

'It was probably some layabout afraid of doing a decent day's work,' said Philip Grigson. 'On social security, most likely, and now he's set up for months.'

'It might be an ex-convict,' suggested Robbie, and was amazed at his ability to discuss the matter as though he was not connected with it. If that woman had not been hurt, how would he feel now? Triumphant, because he had taken the money and got away with it?

But he had never meant to take the money. Something had gone wrong when he entered the bank, some devil had taken him over.

Mr Duncan from head office came down in the morning and spent some time talking to Philip Grigson in the manager's office. They sent for Robbie, and consulted him about general morale among the staff. Robbie said that everyone seemed remarkably calm and undismayed by the incident.

'It would take more than a petty thief to upset Wendy Lomax,' he said.

'Hardly a petty thief, Mr Robinson, since he was armed, and took over three thousand pounds,' said Mr Duncan reprovingly.

Mr Duncan took Philip Grigson off to lunch at the

Red Lion, and among other matters they discussed sending flowers from the bank to Mrs Jordan in hospital. In the end they decided not to do so for the present, as she might be too badly hurt to notice. If she died, a wreath was to be sent and someone from the bank must attend the funeral.

'Mr Robinson,' suggested Mr Duncan. 'He would be appropriate.'

Philip agreed, and looked smug when Mr Duncan commended him on his handling of the affair. The evening had gone well, too: Dawn Smyth's mother had thought it terrible that he should have had such an experience that afternoon. Philip had implied that he had had direct contact with the armed raider and had been instrumental in calming the resulting staff hysteria.

After lunch, Mr Duncan returned to head office, and Philip drove back to the bank confident that it would not be long before he became a manager.

That evening, as they left the bank, Robbie offered once more to drive Wendy home, and she accepted, though she said it must take him out of his way.

They walked together round the corner to his car.

'The red Renault was picked up here last night,' she told him. 'It's a wonder you didn't see it, when you were coming back yourself.'

'Yes, isn't it?' said Robbie. 'But I was just walking along in an ordinary way – I'd have thought nothing of it if I had seen it. Probably I was too late.'

'Probably,' said Wendy.

Robbie wondered how she knew about the car; he decided not to ask her. It might have been in the paper. Instead, he suggested dinner.

'But haven't you got to go home, Robbie?' Wendy asked. 'Aren't you expected?'

'My wife's always out on Thursdays,' said Robbie. 'She

goes to her other shop and has something to eat with the woman who manages it, after they close.'

So Wendy accepted. Robbie said he would come back and collect her at seven o'clock.

He wanted to go home to change his shirt and shave, and to telephone the hospital again.

'There was a raid at Robbie's bank yesterday,' Isabel told Beryl.

'Was that Robbie's bank? I read about it in the *Mail*,' said Beryl. 'Did he have a go at the robbers?'

'There was only one of them, and of course he didn't. Can you imagine it?' answered Isabel. 'He was out at lunch so he missed the whole thing. Typical.'

Beryl loved the evenings when Isabel came to dinner. She planned the menu carefully, and kept a record, so that particular dishes were not repeated too often, shopping for special delicacies. Isabel was not deceived by the nonchalance with which these meals were served; she knew the care and thought that had gone into their preparation and she thoroughly enjoyed the results. It was very pleasant to sit by Beryl's open log fire with a stiff gin and tonic, talking over the day. Both women knew a lot about the private lives of their regular customers; much could be learned from the impulsive purchase of an expensive outfit as an antidote to depression. There were bad payers among the most respected members of local society, and well-to-do ladies who returned a dress a week after buying it, with the complaint that their husbands had not liked it, when the garment showed by traces of powder that it had been worn; the function for which it was bought was now over and the dress of no more interest.

'I've never understood how you and Robbie came to

get married,' said Beryl. 'He can never have been much to look at.'

'He was rather pathetic,' said Isabel. 'He seemed to need looking after. I felt motherly towards him. It wore off.' She did not like to recall their intimate moments before it had. She had tolerated his inexperienced overtures at first as one would endure the affectionate scufflings of a puppy, but soon his diffident ardour had become wearisome. Sex was greatly overrated, in Isabel's opinion. 'His mother died when he was just a child,' she added.

'If you'd had children – ' Beryl hazarded.

'Robbie couldn't even do that,' said Isabel.

'But what was my wife doing in Blewton? I don't understand.'

James Jordan sat in Detective Inspector Thomas's office at Blewton Central Police Station, tired and worried after his hasty flight home and the journey in a police car to the hospital, where Helen had opened her eyes to look at him in a bewildered way and then immediately relapsed into unconsciousness.

'You don't know?' asked Thomas.

'It's a mystery to me,' said Jordan. 'She took me to the airport and I thought she was going straight to the studio.'

Thomas and Detective Sergeant Briscoe glanced at one another. Helen Jordan's employers had already told the police that she had asked for Wednesday off. She had put in a lot of extra time lately and was quite entitled to it. There was an obvious explanation: her husband was out of the country and she was making the most of it.

'You've no family at home, Mr Jordan,' stated Thomas.

'No. My daughter's in Paris with a family, learning French, and my son is in Canada,' said James Jordan.

'So with you away, your wife would have no household duties to keep her at home.'

'No – no, but if she wasn't going to work for some reason, she'd have told me,' said Jordan. 'And she doesn't know anyone in Blewton.'

'Are you sure?'

'Yes.'

Thomas thought he would leave the other man to find out for himself that a wife could have friends her husband knew nothing about, as he had discovered himself in the most painful manner.

'She'll soon be well enough to explain,' he said. The solution to this domestic puzzle was unlikely to lead to the capture of the bank raider. 'We hope she'll be able to tell us a bit about this villain we're after. She may have had a look at him.'

'She won't have seen any more than the people in the bank, will she?' asked Jordan.

'Possibly not – but there may have been something,' said Thomas.

'I can't understand her leaving the keys in the car,' said Jordan. 'She's not usually so careless.'

But she was behaving out of character already, in being in Blewton at all, thought Thomas. At least she was lunching alone in the Copper Kettle; that had been confirmed by the waitress.

'You'd be surprised how many people do it, Mr Jordan,' he said. 'She may have just forgotten that one time.'

'It's automatic, locking the car and taking the key,' muttered Jordan.

'To some people,' said Thomas. 'Hasn't your wife ever rushed back into the house when you've been going out somewhere to make sure she's switched off the iron, or the stove? Of course, she has. That's automatic, to her. The car keys less so, perhaps.'

Jordan did not reply to this observation, and Thomas went on.

'Well now, Mr Jordan, we want to keep quiet about your wife's condition. If this villain we're after thinks she's critically injured, he may panic and do something silly which will help us to find him. He'd be facing a manslaughter charge, at best, if she'd been fatally hurt.'

'It's no thanks to him that she wasn't,' said Jordan angrily.

'Quite, and I mean to catch him,' said Thomas. 'Don't forget, he held up a woman in the bank with a gun, too. We don't want to have him around, ready to do it again.'

'I'm glad to hear you talk like that, Inspector,' said Jordan. 'Everyone's too soft with these people, nowadays.'

'Well, first we've got to find him,' said Thomas. 'So will you help in our little deception? Just keep quiet about your wife – say that her condition's unchanged. That should do for friends.'

'What about my son and daughter?'

'Do they know about her accident?'

'Not yet. I was going to telephone them. They might see a report in the paper – I don't know if they see the English papers very often, but even if they don't, someone else might read about it and tell them.'

'That's true. Well, would you explain? Tell them she's all right and will soon be fit to go home but that we're keeping that to ourselves for the moment.'

'Very well.'

'You'll be spending the night in Blewton?'

'Yes – I suppose so. I hadn't really thought,' said Jordan. 'I suppose I can have the car back?'

'Not yet, Mr Jordan, I'm afraid. The lab has still got it – they're working on it. We should be able to let you have it soon, though – maybe tomorrow. We'll run you to a hotel – there are several in town, I think you'd find the Royal suitable. It's very central.' He stood up. 'I'm very sorry about all this, Mr Jordan.'

'So am I,' said James Jordan. 'So am I, Inspector.'

Wilfred Hunt reported the loss of his shotgun on Thursday. In the opinion of the Harbington police, the cowman's son Barry was the obvious person to have taken it. He knew of its existence; he knew that the house was often left unlocked. He could have found the keys, if he had time to search without fear of interruption. Some people would pay well for such a weapon; it might be in London by now.

There were no fingerprints to prove that Barry had done it. There were Wilfred's, on the drawer and the keys; no one else's. Wilfred thought it strange that his secretary's were not on the drawer; even Robbie might have opened it, looking for paper clips or the stapler, which were kept there. It seemed to prove that the thief had come after Robbie's visit on the Saturday.

'I tell you, I don't know anything about it,' said Barry, grilled by a sergeant while a constable took down a report of their interview.

They searched his room. Barry made no protest; it was no use, they'd soon get a warrant.

'You'll not find it,' he said.

'You've passed it on – sold it, most likely,' said the sergeant.

'I don't know anything about it,' Barry repeated.

'You knew Mr Hunt had it?'

'Course I did. Everyone knows farmers has guns,' said Barry. 'For the vermin.'

'You like shooting. You've got an air rifle.'

'Well? What about it?'

'Not much good for hares and that, is it?'

'You don't go shooting hares now,' said Barry with scorn. 'Not when they're mating.'

'Look son, tell us what you did with it and we'll play it cool,' said the sergeant, dropping the tough tack.

'I can't, when I didn't do a bloody thing,' said the boy.

In the end they had to let him go. He went straight out to the yard and picked up a large stone which he aimed at the windscreen of Wilfred's Land-Rover. But he did not throw it. He walked down the path with the stone in his hand and threw it at the farm kitchen window instead. It landed on the table, knocking off a bowl and two cups that May had been using for baking, and giving her a bad fright.

Helen Jordan had come to Blewton for a funeral. She had seen the notice of Hugo's death in the paper on Monday, and had decided to go. James's trip abroad made it easy for her to take the day off and go down to the country without his knowledge.

It had been an austere service, though Blewton's crematorium had a human organist who had played Bach, with no change in volume, not canned accompaniment. Hugo's coffin, surprisingly small, had vanished behind velvet curtains in the manner of a cinema screen. His widow and their two sons, with wives and children, had occupied the front pews. Helen had worked out who they all were as she stood apart from the other mourners watching them arrive, while the group attending the previous funeral departed from the chapel by another door. It was the best way, she thought: quick flames; no tombstone; but a conveyor-belt operation.

There were a number of elderly men in dark suits and black ties among the congregation. A pretty girl with long blonde hair was weeping: that must be Hugo's grand-daughter.

I loved him too, Helen told her silently.

In the years since her marriage she had met him five times, for lunch at his London club. The last time was four years ago, when he had looked old and frail. After he retired he had moved to the country near Blewton, where he pottered in his garden, and most surprisingly kept bees. Helen had been his secretary, and he had seduced her in the traditional way; there had been others before her, and some afterwards, but she knew that she had been special. Perhaps, in a sense, though it made their relationship sound incestuous, he had seen in her the daughter he had never had, she sometimes thought. She would never forget him. He was her only lover, apart from her husband, and he had wakened her to tenderness. When she met James, she had known quite soon that she wanted to marry him, and they had been happy. But James had never known about Hugo, and he therefore would not understand why she wanted to say good-bye. Before they married, she had wanted to tell him about this one romance, but he had said nothing about his own earlier experiences and had seemed to assume that any she might have had were trivial. In those days there had been no pill and no permissive code of conduct that had to be accepted even if it was not condoned. In the end, Helen had left it. The affair ended when she met James and Hugo had never attempted to resume it. He had given her a fat cheque, and kept in touch, wanting to be sure that she was happy and that things were going well for her. He was fond of his wife, she knew; that aspect of it all had been hard to understand at the time, but now, with the ambivalence of her own feelings, she felt less puzzled.

A policeman had come to see her about the accident, but she had not been able to tell him much. When she told him that she had been to a funeral, he had not reproved her for forgetting the car keys.

'I expect you were upset,' he said, and asked whose funeral and when.

'Why do you want to know?' she asked.

'We just like to be sure,' he said. 'It's routine. We check everything.'

It was strange that she had not told her husband she was going to a funeral.

Arriving at the bank on Friday morning after their evening out, Robbie thought, as he greeted Wendy, how extraordinary it was that the fearful act he had committed had drawn them together. They had spent a very pleasant evening, although when he rang the hospital, assuming his gruff snarl, he had been told that Mrs Jordan's condition was still unchanged.

Wendy had been wearing a black dress which, though nothing special in itself, as he knew from his experience of the stock at Caprice, made her look younger and slimmer. She wore her hair loosely – he did not realize that it had been washed and swiftly blown dry since they parted earlier – and there was a hint of some rather nice scent about her. He wondered what Isabel would think if she could see him dining out with this pleasant girl, and thought that she would simply laugh. True, Wendy was not Angela: she was not the sort of girl men stared at; she was not the type one thought of as a mistress.

Yet perhaps she might become one.

He pushed the idea away, frightened of it, while they chose their veal dishes. Wendy glanced at her watch when he took her home and said it was late, so she would not ask him in. Robbie felt some disappointment, but a touch of relief too. He needed time to think things out.

Greatly daring, he kissed her cheek, and felt her lips warm and soft on his own face. His heart pounded.

On the way back to Harbington he stopped at a call box to ring up the hospital again, but there was no news about Mrs Jordan. Because he had telephoned so late, and because his voice sounded strange to the girl who took the call, she mentioned it.

The night sister in charge of Helen Jordan decided to tell the police; as they wanted the truth about the injured woman's condition concealed for the present, they might be interested in inquirers. They were very interested when they heard that several calls had been made since the incident. When Robbie rang up again on his way to the bank on Friday, that was reported too.

By Friday afternoon, when nothing more had happened, Philip Grigson said that he thought the police were being disgracefully slow in making an arrest.

'He'll get away with it, and do it again,' said Philip.

'I don't see how you expect them to find him so quickly,' said Wendy. 'They've nothing to go on. He left no clues here and he was disguised. And we don't know the numbers of the notes.'

'He's probably living it up on the Costa Brava by now,' said Robbie.

It was strange: he could talk about the robber as if he really was another man.

Philip decided to ring up the police, to see if they had anything to report; then he could tell head office that he had done so, to show that he was alert, though powerless. On Monday the manager would be back and his brief reign ended.

There wasn't much time for talk, however, as Friday was always very busy.

Robbie waylaid Wendy again that evening and took her home. She was going to her evening class, she told him: ancient history. She was interested in Greece and had been to Athens. She was hoping to go to Crete in the summer. All her spare money went on travel.

'What about tomorrow?' Robbie asked. 'Are you busy?'

'In the evening, do you mean?'

Robbie had been thinking of the evening, but when she said that he realized that it was Saturday. There was no work for either of them, but Isabel would be safely in Caprice. He must do the books in the morning, but there was no point in working in the garden, since soon it would be his no more.

'Well – why don't we have a day out?' he said boldly. 'Or an afternoon, at least? If it's a nice day we could go for a run in the country somewhere – have tea – would you like that?' She looked the sort of girl who would enjoy a country walk.

'That would be lovely,' said Wendy with enthusiasm, not sparing a thought for Isabel. Weekends hung heavy now; she had lost touch with many of her friends while she was tied up with Terry and though she was trying to pick up the threads again, she spent a lot of time alone; it was still too early for tennis, which she intended to take up again. Her plans for tomorrow were a visit to the launderette and then perhaps a cinema, if there was anything on worth seeing.

'I'll come about two-fifteen,' said Robbie.

'All right.'

Wendy supposed his Saturdays were rather solitary too. It was a pity. He was really very nice.

8

Helen Jordan had been badly concussed and had broken two ribs; she was covered in cuts and bruises and her face was grazed, so that she looked a somewhat sorry spectacle to her husband as he sat by her bed on Saturday morning wondering if she would soon be able to explain what had happened. She had had moments of consciousness, but these had not lasted long, and he thought she was unaware of his dutiful presence beside her when he should be pursuing export orders in Germany.

A nurse had brought him a cup of coffee. He had just finished it when he saw Helen's eyes regarding him.

'Hullo, James,' she said. 'What are you doing here? You should be in Düsseldorf.'

'I came back, of course, as soon as I heard about your accident,' said James. 'I was here all day yesterday.'

'What day is it?' asked Helen. She tried to raise herself and winced as the pain in her ribs caught her. 'I don't remember,' she added. But she felt clear-headed, for the first time, and she could remember seeing a man with a beard jump into the Renault. The rest was a blur.

'It's Saturday,' James said. 'And you're in Blewton General Hospital. Whatever were you doing in Blewton, Helen?'

'Saturday! But – but it was Wednesday!' Helen exclaimed.

She had vague memories of nurses tending her and

coaxing her to drink. There was a man, too, who had asked questions. A policeman? She didn't think she had answered very sensibly.

'The car! Oh James, I'm sorry! It was stolen,' she said. 'Have they got it back?'

'Yes.'

'Was it damaged?'

'No, not at all.' James was about to ask her what on earth she was thinking of, leaving the keys in it, when she forestalled him.

'I left the keys in it. I suddenly remembered, when I was having lunch in that café. I couldn't find them in my bag when I paid the bill. Then I saw that man get into the car. I thought, what a cheek, and then – did he hit me? I don't remember any more. I think I made a dive for the car.'

'Yes, he did hit you,' said James. 'He'd just robbed a bank.'

'What?'

'That's right. He'd robbed the bank just a few doors down from the café you were in. He got away in the Renault.'

'He didn't hit me on purpose, did he?' asked Helen.

'No one seems to know. I don't suppose he was too particular,' said James. 'He had a gun, in the bank.'

'Was anyone hurt?'

'No. Only you.'

'Well, that's something.'

'You'll have to talk to the police,' said James. 'Now you've come round properly. They did have a police-woman on duty here waiting for you to come round, but she seems to have gone – got more important things to do, I suppose. They'll want to know, though.'

'I can't tell them much,' said Helen. 'I just saw a man – with a beard and wearing a cap, and I think he'd got dark

78

glasses on. Yes, he had. It was a ginger beard,' she added.

'Before I call the police station, what on earth were you doing in Blewton?' James asked.

Helen sighed.

'I'll tell you,' she said. 'But somehow I don't think you're going to understand.'

She could tell he was very angry already: angry because he had had to come home from an important trip, and angry because she was not where he expected her to be. His anger was, she realized, partly relief because she was not seriously hurt. She had flown at the children, in the past, when they had come home later than expected and she had begun to worry about them. Relief made one do this. All the same, he wasn't in the best possible mood to hear about Hugo.

'Let's get the police bit over first,' she cravenly said.

Robbie zipped through Caprice's books on Saturday morning, and put in an hour on Wendy's coffee table too. At eleven o'clock he lifted the telephone to call the hospital, then thought better of it and replaced the receiver. A call box would be safer: he could be ringing from any where.

He walked along the road to the box on the corner and rang the hospital, adopting the same gruff voice. He received the same message as before: Mrs Jordan's condition was unchanged.

As instructed, the hospital noted the time of the call and passed the information on.

He was mad to be setting out with Wendy on an afternoon's enjoyment, Robbie thought, when a woman lay critically ill in hospital because of him, and might die. He had stolen over three thousand pounds from the bank that he had served loyally for most of his adult life; and here he was, off for a day in the country. Moreover, he was meeting a woman who wasn't his wife.

You know perfectly well that Isabel wouldn't go with you if you asked her, Robbie told himself. And you'd hate it, with her. You hate being with her. You hate her.

It was true. She had made him her creature, a thing worth no more than his ability to tot up accounts and balance books, and do repairs about the place. Now, when it was too late, Robbie recognized how pathetic he must have seemed as a young man; and how pathetic, in fact, he had been, to let himself be picked up and swamped like this by Isabel. With hindsight, Robbie saw very clearly how it had happened: he was green and she was desperate to acquire a husband. Girls were less desperate on that score today, he thought, though most of them did still seem to want to marry and have children. Folk made brief excursions into contact with other people, brushing their lives peripherally, but were really alone; everyone was, in the end.

Now he was to brush against Wendy. Why not just make the most of what ensued? Plenty of men took out women who were not their wives, or if they did not do that, they had taken out plenty of women before they married. Robbie had done neither, and he was going to do it now before it was too late: before he got too old, and before he was caught for the robbery.

But he wouldn't be caught. He was the last man who would ever be suspected. He had no alibi for the time of the raid, but everyone knew he walked in the recreation ground in his lunch hour. There was the money to be thought about, too: all three thousand pounds of it. He could spend it on Wendy: spread out over several years, it could buy them several exotic holidays. He must not splash it around recklessly; that would lead to speculation about how he could afford such extravagance. But at the thought of using money which belonged to the bank, he was uneasy. His job, all these years, had been to look after that money.

He parked outside the house where Wendy had her room and opened the front door. The stairs were covered in worn matting. He walked briskly up them and administered a sharp rap to her door.

Wendy was ready. She wore trousers and a padded anorak. Robbie was glad he had assembled his country garb, such as it was – a thick polo sweater and a light anorak he used for holidays. He and Isabel no longer went on holiday together. For a few years they had tried it, and had been to Spain and Yugoslavia. Isabel, immense in a swimsuit, had sunned herself at the poolside while Robbie, who burned easily, lay under the shade of a beach umbrella reading. There had been other couples to chat to in the hotel, and Robbie had enjoyed that; Isabel was at least diluted. Sometimes, seeing Isabel, who never swam, walking around the pool, Robbie would will her to fall in; but someone would certainly rescue her. He dreamed of pushing her in on a dark night.

Now she took a few days off at a time and went to London to fashion shows, and once for a long weekend to Bath with Beryl. The two women talked of going abroad together but felt that one of them must be at hand for the business. They had good assistants now, however, in both shops, and would probably soon decide that things could be left for a fortnight.

Robbie spent most of his holidays working on improvements at 49 Claremont Terrace, or simply enjoying having the house to himself while Isabel was in the shop. He had not thought seriously of going away alone.

The sun came out as Robbie and Wendy drove northwards. He turned off the main road and they went through small villages with houses built of old stone, some with thatched roofs like warm hats and others topped by mellow tiles. Pale, timid wisps of green showed in the hedges and the willow trees carried early buds on their long boughs, like tresses of yellow hair.

They found a museum in a small town, and wandered about looking at displays of ancient weapons and cooking pots. There was an exhibition of old lace, and the ivory bobbins and padded cushions used to make it. Wendy said she would like to learn how to do it. She gazed at the intricate detail, leaning on the showcase, and Robbie leaned on it too so that their elbows touched. She did not move away at all hastily.

They had tea in a thatched cottage with a low, beamed ceiling. A tall, thin woman in a flowered overall served them with scones and clotted cream. Robbie could not remember having tea in a place like this for years. Tea did not feature in his life with Isabel.

'Your wife has to work on Saturdays,' Wendy said, spreading cream.

'Yes.'

'Your wife,' she tried again. She had been very conscious of his elbow touching hers, and had taken care not to move away for several seconds. He had put his hand under her arm to help her into the car, too, and had most carefully helped her off with her anorak as they settled to their tea.

'Isabel's quite a lot older than I am,' said Robbie, and his voice was harsh. 'I was very young when we got married. We don't have a lot in common. She's very wrapped up in her business. She's very successful,' he added, to be fair.

We're two of the walking wounded, thought Wendy.

'I see,' she said. 'Have another scone.'

James Jordan returned to Wimbledon on Saturday evening. The police had released the Renault; they wanted him to come back the next day because if he went home for long the press would realize that Helen was recovering. A small paragraph tucked away in some of the dailies mentioned that her condition was unchanged, but a political kidnapping in Italy was taking the headlines and there was not much space for a story where the trail seemed to have grown cold. If she died, that would be different.

James could not get over the tale Helen had told him about the old man who had been her lover. He was quite appalled.

'A man old enough to be your father,' he had said in disgust.

'He wasn't old then, James, though it's true he was old enough to be my father. He was about the age you are now. And I hadn't met you.'

But James was shocked.

'All these years,' he said. 'All these years I've loved an illusion.'

'Oh, James, be reasonable,' Helen said. 'As for Hugo – I'm sure you fancy young girls – I've seen you looking at them – Ginny's friends – and I've told you, it was before we met.'

She was too weak to argue, and she wept as he drove away.

May had wanted to telephone the police after the kitchen window had been broken, but Wilfred would not agree.

'It's Barry. The police won't have believed him about the gun,' he said.

'Do you believe him?' May asked. The stone – a large one – had only just missed her, and if it had struck her she might have been quite badly hurt. There was the shower of broken glass, too, which could have caused injury, flying into the room.

'I do,' said Wilfred. 'Oddly enough. But I've no idea who can have taken it. It's my fault for leaving the place open to everyone.' But they always had. The farmworkers came in and out, and the family. 'The police must have been too heavy on Barry,' Wilfred added. 'I'll see him. If he apologizes, and mends the window we'll say no more about it.'

'You're probably right,' said May. 'If the boy isn't believed he'll begin to think he may as well do a few of the things he's accused of. But Barry has always been a good lad.'

'He is – he's got some rum friends, though,' said Wilfred.

Barry, confronted, admitted what he had done.

'I was mad at that sergeant,' he said. 'He wouldn't believe I hadn't nicked that gun.'

'Well, breaking a window and causing a lot of damage – perhaps even hurting someone, you might have done that – isn't going to make anyone more likely to think you're telling the truth, is it?' Wilfred asked.

'Suppose not,' muttered Barry.

'We'll forget about this, but you'll pay for the repair – in fact, you can put the window back yourself on Saturday morning,' said Wilfred. The lad worked for a builder, didn't he? Then let him put some of his trade into practice.

Until Saturday, the Hunts endured a kitchen window patched up with cardboard and sellotape. Barry mended it in the morning. He knew the punishment was just but he bitterly resented Wilfred's intended kindness: he was sure, too, that the police would go on leaning on him about the gun until it was found. And he didn't see how it could be.

That afternoon, riding his motorbike, he sat on the tail of a family saloon heading innocently for a safari park; Barry was going to meet some friends, and he was impatient, since half the day was over already. With his engine snorting behind the car, he waited for a chance to overtake. The man driving the saloon, a father of three, with all his family in the car and their picnic tea, could see the scarved and helmeted figure in his mirror, much too close, and he knew it was there when he saw two cars approaching, one overtaking another. He had to brake, or there would be a head-on collision, and if he braked the youngster behind him would cannon into them.

He braked slightly and pulled to the left, though he was already well to his side of the road. He caught the kerb edge and his car went into a spin. Barry zoomed on, and the overtaking car pulled back to its proper position. The driver of the family car just managed to regain control without leaving the road.

Barry rode on, regardless.

As they drove back towards Blewton, Robbie tried to think of a plan. What would another man do now, one who had been around? If he took Wendy to a restaurant – perhaps stopped at one on their way – he would simply deliver her to her door again, and get no further. Not that he was certain he had the nerve to advance; it would depend upon her; the slightest rebuff and Robbie knew he would flee. But if what one heard was true, girls were all on the pill these days and took it as natural to round off an evening in bed. Robbie found it hard to believe that Wendy acted so indiscriminately, but unless he made the opportunity he would never find out how she would react to him.

'What about dinner?' he asked. 'Where would you like

to go? I believe the Riverside Hotel is nice.'

Wendy said at once, 'It's far too smart for me to go there dressed like this. Why don't you come back to my place? We could get something at a take-away place – there's a Chinese one near me.'

'Good idea,' said Robbie, he hoped calmly, as his heart soared. 'I'll get some wine on the way.'

He bought two bottles of claret; one might well not be enough. Wendy raised her eyebrows as he carried them back to the car, smiling.

'Two,' she said.

'If we don't drink them both tonight, there'll be another time,' Robbie said, looking, she thought, quite debonair and really not at all old. He was much better company than an arrogant young man like Philip Grigson, and he had been very solicitous for her comfort, much more than Terry ever had been.

They spent some time at the Chinese take-away place choosing the right mix. Wendy seemed to know quite a lot about Chinese food but Robbie was almost totally ignorant; she seemed, also, to be a regular customer. Robbie wondered who else she entertained with spare ribs and fried rice.

When they got back, Wendy put the containers of food into the oven to keep warm while she laid the table and found glasses. Robbie went down to the bathroom on the floor below. It was a narrow, gloomy room with a brown lino floor and a white enamel bath that had a long brown stain under the hot tap. He thought of his own little shower room with its bright tiles. A proper mistress should live in appropriate style, he reflected. He could give her an allowance from his salary, if he left Isabel. She wouldn't miss his contribution to their expenses; she was always saying how insignificant it was.

Wendy had bought a new bottle of sherry and they

started with that. She put a pile of records on the record player and turned out all the lights except the standard lamp in the corner. There were two tall blue candles on the small dinner table. With the reflection from them, and with the glow from the gas fire, it was snug. Robbie sat with his sherry in the larger chair and wondered how to begin.

It started during the meal. Their knees touched under the table and Wendy did not move her leg away. Robbie felt an excitement he had not known for years, perhaps had never truly known, because this time he was aware of what was happening. He did not know what to say to Wendy but that did not seem to matter. She chattered about her mother's home in Scotland, with the farmer she had met on a cruise.

'I think he had gone on it to find a wife after his own died,' she said. 'I was very worried, at first, about my mother. But she seems happy. I quite like my stepfather.'

Robbie described the death of his own mother when he was a child. They were both semi-orphans, and it was a bond. When they had finished eating there was still some wine left in the first bottle. They stacked the plates in the sink behind the curtain, and put the foil containers in the garbage bin; with this sort of meal there was very little washing up. Then they wandered back towards the fire and the nylon sheepskin rug on the hearth. Robbie topped up their glasses and sipped from his. Then he put it down. He could not kiss her with it in his hand.

Wendy made it all very easy.

9

'You look terrible,' Isabel said when she came downstairs on Sunday morning to do her weekly patrol. After her leisurely rest-day breakfast in bed, she would descend and stroll round the house with a fresh cup of coffee in her hand, deciding what must be done by the cleaning woman the following week, and if there were any particular tasks for Robbie. She would go back to bed then, read the Sunday paper, and remain there until Robbie was out washing the cars or, if the weather was wet and he had to leave them, in his workshop. She only glanced at Robbie when he put down her tray if she wanted to utter some command.

Robbie did feel tired, it was true, but he was elated. He had made successful love – and it was a sort of love – to Wendy not once but twice during the night, only leaving her at three in the morning. It required a supreme effort to go then but he made it; if he succumbed to slumber how would she explain his presence in the morning to the other tenants? They had clung together on her divan, the duvet pulled over them, in the warm glow of the gas fire, and he whispered to her that he had never known such bliss in his life.

At one point in the night, while they rested, they had an interesting discussion. He had told her she need not be worried; he was infertile. 'How do you know?' Wendy asked at once. 'Did you have a test?'

He had not, but Isabel knew that their inability to have children was not her fault.

'How can she be so sure?' demanded Wendy. 'Has she had one?'

'Of course not,' said Robbie, shocked.

'Well, she can't know, then,' said Wendy, and added, for she knew he needed encouragement. 'There's nothing wrong with your performance, Robbie.'

These words had an instant effect on Robbie.

'It was never like this with Isabel,' he murmured into her neck, at one point.

It was a sort of madness, he thought, when he was once again in his own bed at 49 Claremont Terrace, but it was wonderful. With one wild act he had broken out of his timid acceptance of the half life he had lived all these years. Briefly, even the woman lying in hospital was forgotten.

But he ached in unusual places when he got up on Sunday morning, and his lips felt bruised. It would be as well to let a day or two pass before he performed those magic but unaccustomed movements again. He did not answer Isabel's remark, but poured himself another cup of black coffee, and when he had drunk that, he went out to wash the cars.

He gave Charlie the fire engine that morning, and, after some thought, the toy pistol. That was the safest way of getting rid of it. He locked the rest of the things he had used in the robbery back in the cupboard.

Charlie's mother came out to speak to him. She was a tall, thin girl with slim hips and legs that looked as if they had been poured into her tight jeans. With her corkscrew curls of blonde hair she looked, Robbie thought, about fourteen. Her small, round breasts thrust out a skimpy sweater. Robbie did not remember noticing them before.

'You shouldn't keep giving Charlie presents,' she said. 'He likes helping you.'

'I like to give him things,' said Robbie. 'I get most of them with coupons, you know.'

'Well – don't spoil him,' said the girl, who was thankful to have her son so usefully occupied. She went back to her husband. 'Old Robbie next door gave me quite a look just now,' she said. 'Never thought he had it in him.'

'Watch it, love,' said her husband. 'Middle-aged lust can be a terrible thing when it starts to stalk the streets.'

'Where's lunch?' Isabel asked later, when there seemed to be no sign of roasting meat or vegetables boiling.

'Make your own if you want some,' said Robbie. 'I'm going out,' and he drove off to The Bell at Warburton, where he had roast beef and Yorkshire pudding. Chinese food, though satisfying at the time, did not sustain.

When he returned, he could hear the radio on in the sitting room. Isabel must be in there, reading *Vogue* or *Harpers*, a thing she often did on Sunday afternoons. There was a smell of baking: scones, he thought, sniffing. That meant Beryl was coming to tea.

Robbie crept upstairs to his room without being heard. There, he flung himself on his bed and closed his eyes, to conjure images of the night before. In a few minutes he fell into an exhausted sleep.

He slept for nearly two hours. Yawning, stretching, he looked out of his attic window at the garden. What a lot of work he should be doing in it, if he were not leaving. It would be nice if he could stay here, at the top of the house, on his own, without Isabel.

He went downstairs and made himself some tea. The trolley, with Isabel's and Beryl's used cups and plates on it, stood in a corner of the kitchen. There were some shortbread biscuits on a plate but either Isabel had put away whatever she had baked or it had all been eaten.

Robbie did not want anything she had touched: the biscuits, factory made, were impersonal.

He took a large mug of tea and four biscuits out to his shed, where he settled down to work at Wendy's coffee table.

Some time later he heard Isabel calling.

Let her call, he thought, planing a leg. He did not answer, and after some minutes she came to the door.

'Didn't you hear me?' she demanded. 'You're wanted on the telephone. It's that farmer friend of yours. He said it was very important, about some gun he's lost. I told him you wouldn't know one end of a gun from another but he insists on speaking to you.'

She was already walking away while she spoke.

Robbie had forgotten the shotgun, still locked in his cupboard. He followed Isabel up the path to the house. Her dark hair was lacquered into position; her wool two-piece made her body look like a square box. He knew that strong elastic contained her heavy rump. Now he knew, too, that she had never had any sexual allure, at any rate for him. He had clung to her as a sick man might clutch at a competent nurse.

Wilfred explained what had happened and asked Robbie if he had seen the gun when he was at the house the previous weekend. It was his XXV, he explained, the shortest barrel allowed by the law of the country, twenty-five inches, and he used it mostly for rabbits in woodland.

'I'm sorry, Wilfred,' Robbie lied fluently. 'I didn't look at your guns. It might have been there, or then again, it might not. I wouldn't have noticed. When did you miss it?'

'About ten days ago,' Wilfred said. 'I've told the police, and they think the cowman's son must have taken it, but I'm sure he didn't. He's denied it and I believe him. I'm afraid the police might lean a bit too hard on him if it doesn't turn up.'

'Oh dear,' said Robbie. 'Well, who do you think has taken it?'

'God knows. The place is always open, as you know, and May's been away. It could be some lad passing by.'

'Anything else missing?'

'No.'

'Some casual passer-by would be more likely to look for money, wouldn't he?' said Robbie.

'Yes. But it could be someone after a gun, who knew there'd be one here,' said Wilfred.

Just in time, Robbie realized he must not comment on the keys. The less he seemed to know about Wilfred's habits, the better.

'Sorry I can't be of any help,' he said.

'I didn't think you would be,' said Wilfred. 'It was just a chance. Might help to pinpoint when it happened.'

'You do get a lot of callers, don't you?' Robbie said. Men were always coming with forms, or delivering feed or seed. 'It could have been any of them, couldn't it?'

'Well, if one was a villain, yes,' said Wilfred. 'I suppose the police will talk to them, the regulars, anyway. But it's hard to believe that any of them would do such a thing. Most of them have been coming here some time.'

'You read these extraordinary things in the paper,' Robbie said.

'The police think Barry might have sold it to some scoundrel or other,' said Wilfred. 'Might be the chap that robbed your bank.'

'That was a pistol,' said Robbie.

'Well, he might be part of a gang,' said Wilfred. 'Anyway I expect there are plenty of villains about looking for such things, if we only knew.'

'I expect so,' Robbie agreed.

'Well, sorry to bother you,' said Wilfred.

'That's all right,' Robbie answered. 'Sorry I can't help. I hope it turns up.'

'I don't see how it can,' said Wilfred. 'I'm worried about Barry.'

Robbie had thought vaguely of returning the gun to Wilfred's study some time when the house was empty but it might not be easy to find such a moment, when no one was around to see him. He could dump it somewhere where it would soon be found; there would be nothing to connect him with it in any way. He must just be sure not to leave it where it could be found by someone irresponsible.

He could hear the yak-yak of the two women's voices coming from behind the sitting room door. Perhaps if he wasn't around they'd set up house together: and he might go to Greece with Wendy.

In the evening he walked down the road to the call box on the corner to telephone the hospital.

Wendy slept soundly after Robbie left her in the early hours of Sunday morning, and she rose late, singing to herself as she brewed a mug of instant coffee and poured cereal into a bowl. The plates from their evening meal were in the sink; Robbie had mentioned the washing up, apologetically, as he left. She thought he must be a very nice husband: kind, and so dependable. His home life wasn't very happy, clearly, and she supposed it must be difficult to have a wife who was so much more successful than he was. The business about the baby, or lack of one, had shocked her; extraordinary that Robbie had accepted his wife's verdict without question; no young man would unless his wife had had exhaustive tests. It showed how old he was, or how he had failed to move with the times.

He hadn't seemed old in the night, just endearingly diffident. They were both lonely; there was nothing wrong in offering comfort, of a sort, to one another, and kind Robbie could never cause her any harm.

As she sat in the bus going to visit her friend Ella, who was married to a veterinary surgeon and lived fifteen miles from Blewton, Wendy thought about him, and where their interlude of the night before might lead. They'd have to be very careful, if they went on, not to be discovered by their colleagues at the bank. There was no future in it, but for the present it was consoling; she felt happier than for a long time. Wendy decided not to look ahead.

Her friend Ella met the bus and drove her to the country cottage where she lived with her husband and two small sons. Ella was intrigued about the bank raid and wanted to hear all the details. Wendy told her a little about what had happened, and disclosed that she had been the cashier who was held up at gunpoint.

'Weren't you terrified?' asked Ella.

'There wasn't time to be,' said Wendy. 'It was all over so fast. It was more frightening afterwards, really thinking about it and what might have happened.' And sitting in the police station looking at pictures of known villains to see if she could recognize the raider.

Ella's two sons were playing a chasing game in the garden. They wore scarves round their faces and cowboy hats on their heads, and both had pistols. When the children came in to lunch they laid down their guns on the kitchen sideboard. Idly, Wendy glanced at them. One was shiny, silvery-looking; the other was a dull pewter colour, with a short snout. It was exactly like the gun that had been held in that gloved hand so menacingly four days ago.

Wendy telephoned the police station as soon as she reached home on Sunday evening. Detective Inspector Thomas was there, and she was put through to him.

He listened without interruption while she explained about the toy pistol. Then he said he would come to fetch her and take her back to her friend's house; he wanted to see the weapon.

Wendy expected a police car to arrive outside the house, but Thomas came in an ordinary black Cortina.

'I should have rung you from Ella's,' she said. 'I'm sorry if the delay's going to make a difference. But it seemed so silly! He can't have used a toy gun.'

'He could have,' said Thomas. 'Don't worry, a few hours won't matter very much. It's not as if you thought you'd seen our actual villain.'

'How are you getting on?' Wendy asked.

'To be truthful, it's gone completely cold on us,' said Thomas. 'He can't have picked up another car after he dumped the Renault – there wasn't one stolen anywhere near that area on Wednesday. He must have left another car near the spot where he left the Renault. He probably meant, originally, to run round to it, trusting to the start he had to get away before anyone rushed after him. A young, fit chap, I guess.'

'And he saw the Renault and took it on the spur of the moment?'

'Yes.'

'Did he leave anything in the Renault – fingerprints?'

'No prints – remember the gloves? But we found a wisp of hair that may have come from the beard. That's being tested. We may be able to discover who made it, and from that it's sometimes possible to trace retailers. If a grown man bought a false beard and a toy pistol in the same shop recently, someone may remember.'

'But they could have been bought anywhere in the country,' said Wendy. 'And not in the same shop at all – and not recently.'

'Exactly,' said Thomas.

'Goodness, what a job,' said Wendy.

'I mean to get him,' said Thomas. 'He knocked that woman down and it's no thanks to him she isn't dead,' he added as they turned in at the gate of Ella's cottage.

Ella was extremely surprised to see Wendy back again. The boys were now in bed, but Ella produced the two pistols.

'This is the one.' Wendy pointed it out.

'It came from cereal carton tops,' said Ella promptly. 'Gavin saved them up. We got heartily sick of the stuff, to tell you the truth, by the time he'd enough.'

'I'll have to take it away, I'm afraid,' said Thomas. He pulled three pound notes out of his wallet. 'Will that be enough to get him another? I don't suppose the offer's still on or that you want to save up all over again. What cereal was it? Do you remember?'

'I'll never forget,' said Ella, and told him.

'Will you pretend to Gavin that it's had some sort of accident?' asked Thomas. 'If you tell him the truth he may let it out and we don't want our villain to know we've identified the weapon until we're good and ready.'

Ella sighed.

'I expect I can think of something,' she said.

As they drove back to Blewton, Wendy asked Thomas if he had any children.

'Two boys much the ages of your friend's kids,' said Thomas.

'So that's how you know about the importance of toy pistols?'

'That, and having had one myself at around eight or nine,' said Thomas.

Wendy supposed there was some sort of fund to reimburse Thomas.

'I don't see my boys all that often,' Thomas added. 'I'm divorced. Their mother has married again and she lives near Cambridge.'

'Oh, I'm sorry,' said Wendy.

'It's hard on a woman, being married to a copper,' said Thomas. 'She's left alone a lot.'

'I suppose so.' Thomas certainly seemed to work all round the clock.

On the way home he took her round to the police station where he played her a tape recording of a gruff voice inquiring about Mrs Helen Jordan.

'Was that the same voice as the one you heard in the bank?' he asked.

'Well, I couldn't swear to it,' said Wendy cautiously. 'It sounds a bit odd because of the telephone. But it was very like that.'

'He's been ringing up every day,' said Thomas. 'We're not letting it be known that Mrs Jordan wasn't badly hurt at all.'

'Can you trace the calls?'

'We haven't yet. He uses a telephone box, and he's so quick.'

'At least he's got some sort of conscience,' Wendy said.

'He's worried about himself – what he could be in for, if she'd died,' said Thomas.

He drove her home and dropped her at her door. As she walked upstairs she wondered if he would be going back to the police station again, or if he would be going home, wherever home was now for Detective Inspector Thomas.

10

On Monday Nigel West, the manager at the bank, was back from his Majorcan holiday. He had enjoyed a week of bracing sea air and strong winds, not the sunny warmth he had expected; but the food and drink, and the long nights with Susan, had fortified him for what he would find on his return. He did not, however, expect to learn that his bank had been raided the moment his back was turned.

He spent an hour on Monday morning hearing full reports from everyone about what had happened, and then he had a conference with Philip Grigson, his chief clerk, and with Robbie, in view of his experience.

No more could have been done by anyone, he decided. Inevitably, there was a delay because the alarm had to be relayed to the police by the security system, but a car had arrived eight minutes after the robber left.

'Well, lightning never strikes the same place twice,' said Robbie. 'I expect we'll be safe enough here now.'

Nigel frowned at him.

'Not at all,' he said sharply. 'If other thieves learn whoever did this has got away with it, they may try us.' He twiddled the ballpoint pen he held. 'I'll get on to the police—make sure they really are trying to catch this rogue.'

'I'm sure they are,' said Philip. 'But he left no clues.'

'You can't be sure,' said Nigel. 'In their eyes, three thousand odd pounds is chicken-feed. They're probably not bothering too much. It would be a different matter if the haul had been bigger.'

'I don't think the police reason like that,' said Robbie. 'It's all crime to them.'

'Well, everyone seems to have behaved very well,' allowed Nigel, dismissing them.

Later, he sent for Wendy. She looked none the worse for her adventure; in fact, he thought she looked particularly well this morning. It was lucky that one of the younger, less calm girls, had not been the victim of the hold-up.

Wendy did not tell him about the pistol. She was not sure if Detective Inspector Thomas meant its identification to become public knowledge.

Robbie had noticed Wendy's bright look that morning. He felt bright himself, in spite of – perhaps because of – everything. It was a pity that his and Wendy's lunch hours were staggered, so that he could not invite her to the Copper Kettle, but then if they had not been staggered, she would not have been at the counter during the raid, and he would not have taken her home afterwards. He had brought no sandwiches this morning; there had been no roast to cut for them, and the cheese had run out as he had not shopped on Saturday. He went into the supermarket and bought some more before he had lunch at the Copper Kettle.

Over lamb chops with peas, Robbie finished the *Daily Telegraph* crossword. Then he went for his usual stroll. It was a fine day, though the wind was cold. Daffodils in the recreation ground were in bud, and two boys, truants from school, were riding skateboards down a path. Robbie thought it looked fun; he would have liked to try it himself. More of that sort of activity for young people and there would be less spare energy for mugging old ladies, he felt. At last, staring at a clump of yellow crocuses, he faced what he had tried to dodge all morning: the fact of the woman lying injured in hospital; that morning on the telephone he had been told that her condition was still the same. If she died, he would have killed her, however much of an accident it was.

Wendy went home from the bank alone that evening. They had arranged to meet at the *trattoria* where they had dined before; then, it was implicit, they would go back to her room.

Robbie shaved and changed his shirt in the men's room at the Royal Hotel, then waited in the lounge until it was time to walk round to the restaurant. As he left the hotel, a thickset man with brown hair entered; unknown to Robbie, he was Helen Jordan's husband.

Robbie telephoned the hospital again on the way to the *trattoria*. The message was still the same.

Wendy told him about the toy pistol, while they ate their *gnocchi*.

'So the robber wasn't a hardened criminal, then,' said Robbie.

'You can't say that, Robbie,' Wendy answered. 'He meant me – whoever he pointed it at – to think it was real. It's a crime to do that.'

'How are the police getting on?' Robbie asked. He would not let himself be dismayed by the coincidence which had led Wendy to recognize the pistol. The cereal packet manufacturers were very unlikely to keep a record of where they sent such things.

'I don't think they've got anywhere,' said Wendy. 'There's nothing to go on. He was certainly clever.'

'If that woman dies – ' Robbie said.

'She won't,' Wendy cut in. 'She's not at all badly hurt, luckily. She was concussed, and has some broken ribs and bruises, but it isn't serious. They'll be letting her out of hospital soon. But they're keeping it quiet because someone's been ringing up the hospital twice a day to ask about her. He uses a gruff sort of voice – they've recorded him making his calls and they've tried to trace where they come from, but he uses a call box and it's all too quick. The police played the recording to me yesterday to see if I recognized the voice.'

'And did you?' Robbie hoped his voice stayed calm and steady.

'It sounded the same. I couldn't swear, of course, but it was just like the robber's.'

Robbie did not speak for a few seconds. The woman would not die, but if Wendy had not told him this he would have gone on telephoning, and he might have been caught.

'They'll get him,' he said at last.

'I hope they do,' said Wendy. 'But I'm not sure that they will. They won't be able to keep Mrs Jordan in hospital much longer, and they'll never be able to let her go without the press finding out. He'll stop ringing then, and that's all they've got to go on. They did find a hair from the false beard in the Renault, and they may be able to trace the makers, but the chance of finding out who bought it is pretty slim.'

'He might do another raid,' said Robbie, nonchalantly.

That night was even better than their first. Robbie did not get home until two in the morning. If he kept these late hours up, some neighbour would notice even if Isabel never heard the car, and she would feel gravely insulted if she knew what was happening. But he didn't care about that. He was going to leave her. When the move to the new house was due, Robbie would find himself a flat somewhere – in Blewton, perhaps, nearer to Wendy.

A nice girl like Wendy must want to be married, he thought. Would she consider him? If he didn't rush her, she might, he dreamed.

The thought that the police had recorded his telephone

calls to the hospital was frightening. He knew from his intensive viewing of television that there were all sorts of sophisticated methods for discovering where calls came from. Thank goodness the woman was all right, but even so she had been hurt and there was no escaping the blame for that.

He must get rid of the money. It was the only way to wipe the slate clean. He couldn't ask Wendy, or if she would not have him, some other woman, to share any sort of life with him if this was in the background. He had never intended to take it; he still did not understand what had happened that day to make him go through with the escapade.

On Tuesday morning he took his carrier bags out of the cupboard where he had locked them after the robbery. He checked his disguise. Everything was there.

That evening there was a choral group meeting. Robbie had joined it three years before rather by chance. A former colleague of his from the Harbington branch of the bank had handled arrangements for the booking of the town hall for a concert in aid of the hospital, and then fallen ill. He had asked Robbie to take over the business. Joining the choir in the Crown after the concert, Robbie had envied their camaraderie as they drank beer or cider, port or sherry, according to taste, all laughing and joking. Out in the cold himself, he was drawn to the warmth of others more secure. The suggestion that he should join the singers was made frivolously at first; Robbie did not think he had enough of a voice, though as a boy he had enjoyed singing at school and had learned to read music. Then he thought how scornful Isabel would be; she lacked all musical sense. But if he were to be accepted, it would give him another excuse for evading her, and though she might mock, he could count it an achievement. He decided to audition, and sang 'A wandering minstrel

I' from *The Mikado*, with great feeling if some inaccuracy; he floundered somewhat over the scales and vocal exercises also demanded of him, but had demonstrated his ability to hold a tune and was enrolled. He had improved since then and now he enjoyed the sessions, letting his own voice fuse with those around him, losing himself in the melody.

But that Tuesday evening the two hours of the meeting seemed long, and it was hard to concentrate on *The Desert Song*, excerpts from which were to be given at a charity musical evening, and a French folk song being ambitiously introduced into the repertoire by the choirmaster, who taught music at Harbington's comprehensive school. The group was in some demand to provide light entertainment by those organizing community events in the area.

Robbie made his one drink last a long time at the Crown, but that was normal; he was often teased for his abstemiousness. At last he felt that he could leave, a little earlier than usual, but not a lot; he must not act in any sort of unexpected way. He got into his car in the hotel yard and drove, not home, but to Overtown, thirty miles away. Outside the town he turned off the main road into a lane and there, in the darkness, he put on his disguise: the beard, the wig, the cap and the raincoat. He slipped the dark glasses into his pocket to be worn later as he could not drive in the dark wearing them. Then he went on into the town. It was late, and there was no one about though the street lights were on and some of the shops were illuminated. Robbie knew that his bank's branch was in a quiet part of the main street, between an estate agent's office and a doctor's surgery, and he drove past it into a side road where he left the car among some others which seemed to be parked for the night. He put on the dark glasses and the gloves from the car's locker, and picked up the carrier containing the money from under the passenger's seat where it had spent the evening; then he walked quickly back to the bank where he thrust the carrier through the letter-box. It had a wide opening, but even so it was quite difficult to flatten the banknote bundles out, through the plastic, and force it through. Without a key, he could not use the night safe. The job done, he walked on past the bank and was soon lost in the shadows of another side street. He walked fast, back to the car, completing a circle.

He felt a great sense of relief at having returned the money. The newspaper reports had mentioned the use of a blue carrier bag by the thief, so no Sherlock Holmes would be needed to deduce whence it came.

The crime he had committed was now expunged.

When told what had been received with the mail on Wednesday, the manager of the Overtown branch of the bank first of all telephoned Nigel West at Blewton.

'We think we've got your stolen money,' he said. 'Haven't counted it, in case of prints, but it looks as if it's all there. In a blue carrier.'

'Good God,' exclaimed Nigel.

'We'd better get on to the police. I haven't rung ours yet, but I think we'd better get someone here pretty soon.'

'So do I,' said Nigel. 'You ring yours and I'll get hold of the local inspector who's on the case. Well, would you believe it?'

The two managers exclaimed a little more and decided that they would not tell head office until the police had been, then rang off.

Nigel West immediately telephoned Blewton Central where he spoke to Detective Inspector Thomas, who said he would send a man to Overtown to liaise with the local officers.

Rum, he thought, and pondered Wendy's theory of remorse. But chummy had stopped calling the hospital; there had been no telephone inquiry about Mrs Jordan for twenty-four hours. There was no point in keeping quiet any longer; Thomas rang up the hospital and said they might issue a bulletin if they wished. Newspaper references to the robbery had ceased as no more had happened to fan interest in it. Some mention of Mrs Jordan might spark off a new reaction, and if the news of the money's return was given to the press it might turn out that someone had seen the mystery depositor.

So far, the lab had not been able to trace the makers of the false beard worn by the raider, but when the stolen money was returned, Detective Inspector Thomas started inquiries at shops within a radius of thirty miles which sold such things. If that yielded nothing, he would extend the range, and by then the lab might have been able to be more precise. Few records were kept of such over the counter dealings, but an assistant somewhere might remember the transaction they were after. This was where luck came in, added to the painstaking work of sifting and sorting information. It turned out that false beards were bought fairly frequently for amateur theatricals.

Briscoe returned from Overtown with the news that a wisp of thread had adhered to the carrier bag holding the money; it was brown fibre, and could be from the carpet of a car. There was also a little dust. The samples had gone off to the lab.

'The Overtown law's asking around to see if anyone saw chummy make the drop,' said Briscoe. 'They're checking people who used the night safe that night, to see if they saw anyone near the bank, but they've got a missing kid on their patch. They're a bit short of men.'

'Let's ask the local radio boys to put out an appeal,' said Thomas. 'Might be lucky.'

He'd got no missing child in his area, but in addition to finding the bearded raider he had to deal with several cases of larceny and one of arson.

He'd arranged to see his children at the weekend. Too often before, such plans had had to be cancelled; he wondered if he'd make it this time.

No wonder his wife had got fed up.

The press enjoyed the story about the return of the money. It was easy to surmise that the robber had chosen a different branch so that he need not revisit the scene of the crime, but he had not moved far. The story about the telephone calls to the hospital had leaked, too: 'ROBBER WITH A CONSCIENCE', said one paper, going on to say, 'If Helen had Died, He'd have been a Killer'. Another paper talked of the gentle gunman who inquired about his victim.

'He didn't seem so gentle,' Wendy said, as these efforts were studied in the bank on Thursday. 'He held that gun at me and demanded the money pretty fiercely. I wasn't to know it was a dummy.' The papers knew about the toy pistol now; Wendy supposed Thomas must have decided to tell them. There were times when leaking information was useful, as occasionally law-abiding citizens, stumbling on information, would come forward. Maybe some child's gun was missing: borrowed by its father?

'He must have been seen dumping that carrier in Overtown,' said Philip Grigson. 'You can't walk up to a bank and stuff three thousand pounds through the letter box without being seen. It must have taken a lot of shoving.'

'He'd have been in his disguise,' said Angela Fiske. 'Wouldn't he?'

'Maybe he wore a different one, this time,' said the typist, who was feeling less new in her second week. 'White whiskers, like Santa Claus.'

They speculated about it at odd moments during the day. Returning the money seemed to have made the robber more real to them: humanized him.

Robbie knew that he might have been seen, but he was sure that no one had followed him from the bank to his car, and there was no one about when he drove off.

All that was needed was nerve.

He did not switch channels on the television that evening when he heard Isabel come in. She had been at a meeting called by local tradesmen to consider their latest rates demand, and had had dinner with some of them at the Crown. While she was out, Robbie had telephoned Wendy and talked to her for over half an hour. He had asked her to go away with him for the weekend, saying that it wasn't good for her reputation if he kept leaving her place so late at night.

How old-fashioned he was, she thought, but she found it touching. He didn't know about Terry, who had so often stayed all night.

She demurred at first.

'We've got into this so suddenly, Robbie,' she said.

'If we can have a weekend together, we may know if we want to go on,' said Robbie. 'Or you may. I know about myself.'

Why not, thought Wendy, and agreed.

'I suppose you've been stuck there in front of the television all evening,' Isabel said, entering the sitting room.

Robbie had worked for a while on Wendy's coffee table, but he was very tired and had soon come in; he had dozed in front of the set and in fact it was not switched to a thriller now but to a programme about insects.

He did not answer Isabel.

'You must get all your stuff packed up this weekend,' Isabel went on. 'We're moving the following one, remember. Throw away everything you don't use. There's no point in taking a lot of rubbish.'

'I'm going away next weekend,' said Robbie. He should have added, 'And I'm not coming back,' but he didn't.

'Away? But you never go away,' said Isabel.

'Well, I am now,' said Robbie. 'With a friend,' he added. 'No one you know.'

'You can't go. You've got to pack,' said Isabel.

'I'll do it when I get back,' he said. And then he'd look for a place of his own.

When Isabel went up to her room, she found a Teasmade machine wired up and placed beside her bed. Robbie had finished carrying trays.

Helen Jordan was glad to be at home, but she felt as if she was living with a stranger. James had moved into his dressing room, in order, he said, not to disturb her. She was pleased in a way that she did not have to worry about waking him, when she stirred restlessly during the night, but his aloof politeness to her made her aware that he had not moved merely out of consideration. She was being punished.

The second evening his icy manner was too much for her. She accepted the glass of sherry he gave her, and then said, 'How long is this going on, James? I'm in the doghouse because when I was a young girl a man took me to bed and taught me about tenderness. Do you think you're so wonderful that I'd have learned about it from you?'

'I've always thought our sex life was satisfactory,' said James austerely.

'It is – was. Because I'd learned not to be inhibited – a thing that didn't always come easily to girls of my generation,' said Helen. 'You're a good man, James, but you're not imaginative.'

'I trusted you,' said James.

'I should hope so,' said Helen. 'It had nothing to do with you, James. I hadn't met you then.'

'You should have told me about it.'

'If I had, you'd have called off our marriage, wouldn't you?' Helen said.

He looked at her with a steely eye.

'Probably,' he said. 'You were tarnished,' and he slammed out of the house.

Helen began to laugh. His reaction was archaic. But she was still weak, and after a while she began to cry. Who did he think he was, for God's sake? She hadn't inquired about his activities either before marriage or since; he might well have strayed with a *fräulein* when overseas, but she trusted him not to jeopardize all that they had built up together over so many years. Now it seemed that the structure was so unsoundly based that it could be washed away by the first really serious storm. And it was so pointless. She began to feel that her whole marriage had been built on a false foundation and that the years of family life had been a living lie.

She went upstairs and began to pack. She'd go to her sister's for a few nights and see what happened. She'd tell Pamela the truth, but they'd say she was there because she still felt shaky after the accident. It was true enough. It would give her time to regain some strength, and it would give James time to come to his senses: if he ever did, since their relationship had been based, it seemed on an illusion.

James, drinking his third double gin in a pub, felt himself to be a man betrayed. Nothing would ever be the same again.

I I

Isabel had spent Friday evening as well as Thursday with Beryl. She wanted to tell her affectionate, faithful friend about Robbie's rebellion and the advent of the Teasmade.

'I can't think why you didn't have one years ago,' said Beryl, who did not enjoy the idea of Robbie in his dressing gown entering Isabel's room.

'Oh, I liked him coming in with the tray,' Isabel admitted. 'It kept him in his place. And it gave me a chance to speak to him, if there was something I needed to say. We scarcely meet, you know. Really, it's been quite civilized.'

'Has he come round about the move?'

'No. He's gone away for the weekend, if you please. I don't think he's ever done such a thing before. But he said he'd pack when he gets back.'

'Where's he gone?'

'I don't know – and I didn't ask. The less fuss, the sooner it'll all be over,' Isabel said. 'He's always been like a child. This is just childish temper.'

'You might be better off without him,' Beryl dared to say. It was true that Isabel was moving no nearer to her, but without Robbie around, she could pop over to Harbington any time and have more excuse to do things for Isabel. She'd need help, with no Robbie.

'He's useful,' Isabel said. 'He's always there when I want odd jobs done, and it's useful to have him for the books.'

'We could employ an accountant,' said Beryl. 'We can afford it. And there are handy carpenters around.'

'Not at weekends,' said Isabel. 'It's useful to be able to get things done promptly. Besides, I've looked after him long enough – I expect some return.'

'You're quite conventional, aren't you?' said Beryl. 'You like the appearance of being married.'

'It's not what I like. It's how society works,' said Isabel.

'But the system's breaking down,' said Beryl.

'It's not. People just go their own ways more,' Isabel answered.

But a rebellious Robbie was not something she had had to deal with before, and on Saturday morning she awoke alone in the house. He wouldn't be there to do the books – well, he could make that up one evening. But several times lately he'd come home very late. She'd heard the car, though she said nothing. She slept heavily as a rule, but the unusual sound of Robbie's car arriving when everything else was quiet had roused her. What could he have been doing? Charlie's mother, next door, had commented on it, saying, 'You were late last night, weren't you? Living it up, then?' in a cheery way as Isabel left for the shop and Charlie left for school. Isabel had ignored the remark, though the girl seemed to think they had been somewhere together.

If it was any other man, she'd suspect some woman, but not where Robbie was concerned.

You could get used to things so quickly, Wendy thought. Every day now, at the bank, there was a hidden excitement. She was so used to Robbie's working presence that most of the time she forgot about it, and both of them were too busy with their work to think of much else, but now and then she would smile to herself with secret amusement.

Robbie had changed. He was livelier, often joked with the younger girls, and had quite an argument with Philip Grigson about a customer's complaint over excess charges, proving Philip's pronouncement on the matter wrong, what was more. Wendy felt more cheerful too; the days had ceased to drag. She had been thinking of asking for a transfer even without promotion; things would never change for her in Blewton, she had felt, and a new environment might be stimulating. Then, in a flash, life had altered.

She was already fond of Robbie; otherwise she would never have let things go so far; but now she had developed a great dislike for his wife – almost a horror. That woman had destroyed something essential in him – his self-esteem – and Wendy thought she might help its restoration.

If the weekend away was a failure and she wanted to return to their earlier, merely workaday, relationship, her own trip to Scotland would make it easy to break with him. She could return after the week away and carry on as before, quite casually. She accepted her own share of responsibility for the situation between them; she could have discouraged him at the start, but she hadn't, because she was beginning to fear her own solitude.

'But James is being ridiculous,' said Helen Jordan's sister.

Helen had been given breakfast in bed on Sunday morning. She sat propped against pillows in Pamela's spare room drinking coffee, while her sister sat on the end of the bed idly glancing through the *Observer* as they talked. Outside, Pamela's husband could be heard giving the lawn the first mow of the season, and there was also the thump, thump, of a tennis ball hitting the garage door as Helen's niece practised.

'I know he is,' said Helen.

'Hugo was a lamb,' said Pamela. 'I used to wonder about you and him, but I was never sure.'

'You were too young to know about such things in those days,' said Helen. She moved awkwardly in the bed. 'This rib still hurts like the dickens.'

'Poor old thing,' said Pamela. 'But they do. They take ages to mend. What an ass James is. He's jolly lucky you haven't been off on a few shady weekends.'

'Have you?' asked Helen.

'No, I couldn't. Even if I was tempted, I'm much too fond of dear old Tim to do anything like that,' said Pamela. 'But I can understand how people might. Boredom could make you, for instance.'

'I thought James and I had a good marriage,' Helen said. 'It was hard at first, but now he's doing well and things are easier, and the children seem to know what they want to do and are on the way to doing it. I thought I was happy.'

'You've got a good job. You could manage on your own very well,' said Pamela. 'James may feel threatened. Men do break out in middle age, quite often, and I suppose with him it's taken the form of jealous pique. I wonder how it will hit Tim?'

The prospect of plump, equable Tim breaking out into adultery or jealous rage, or indeed, in any other way, seemed unlikely.

'He might need something, to restore his self-confidence,' Pamela mused. 'Some young girl at the office for instance, like Hugo went after you.'

'There wasn't much wrong with Hugo's self-confidence,' said Helen. 'He just liked women.'

'Well, if Tim gets up to anything like that, I just hope

I never know about it,' said Pamela. 'I'd be furious. What about James? Do you think he spends his evenings alone in Düsseldorf or wherever he goes?'

'I think he's probably too tired to do anything else,' said Helen. 'Those trips are exhausting.'

'Um, yes. Well, he's a prig. He'll be frightened, though, when he finds you've gone. He'll soon come to heel. You stay here as long as you like. You won't be fit to go back to work for some time.'

'That wretched man,' said Helen. 'That robber. It's all his fault.'

'You must have been a bit reckless, getting in his way,' said Pamela. 'You couldn't have stopped him, after all.'

'I couldn't believe what was happening. He'd started the engine and got the car in gear before I knew it. In fact I think he moved off with a jerk, and that's why he hit me. But think – if he'd been going at any speed I'd have been badly hurt. As it was, it felt like a damn great bus hitting me.'

'Well, it was moving, and you struck your head on the kerb, didn't you? That's what knocked you out,' said Pamela. 'Bad luck on the thief, really. He was only pinching money and now he'll have to face a charge of attempted manslaughter, won't he?'

'I hope so,' said Helen. 'If they ever catch him. But for him, none of this trouble with James would have happened.'

'Wouldn't you rather know just how frail your marital craft is?' asked Pamela. 'Better to face it now than when you're ten years older, and feeling a lot less spunky.'

The hotel was by the sea. It had a glassed-in sun lounge with plants in pots, and a main lounge with deep chairs and a television set. The restaurant was papered in mock brocade and was lit by two chandeliers. It was very comfortable and rather expensive. Robbie and Wendy spent very little time in the public rooms; their own room was large, with a balcony overlooking the sea, which was choppy and grey. They reached it late on Friday night: Wendy had cut her ancient history class with only a minor pang.

After breakfast in bed, they took the car into the country where they walked over the downs until it was time to find somewhere for lunch. Robbie had bought various guides, and they found a recommended pub where ham on the bone and game pie were featured. The atmosphere was friendly, and Robbie visibly expanded. Wendy was touched by the change in him; he looked years younger. He wasn't old at all, yet behind his back he had always been known in the bank, since he came there, as Old Robbie.

In the afternoon they poked around various shops looking at things. Wendy liked a picture of a sailing ship; it was an old galleon, a water-colour in soft greys and misty blues with white curling foam. It cost fifty pounds, and Robbie bought it for her.

'But you mustn't, Robbie,' she protested. 'It's much too expensive. I can't let you.'

Robbie thought of the useless trinkets he had bought Isabel over the years. They meant nothing to her.

'You like it, don't you?' he asked.

'I love it,' she said.

'It'll go in your room?'

'Yes. Over the mantelpiece.'

'Well, then.'

'You are a dear,' she said, and when they were back in the car, kissed him warmly.

Robbie felt wonderful. Could it really be that after all these years his life was going to change?

In bed that night he said, 'I'm going to leave Isabel, Wendy. I'm not going with her to the new house. She can please herself what she does about that but she can do it alone.'

This news did startle Wendy; she thought it wiser not to comment.

'If I got a divorce, would you marry me?' he asked her, and then added quickly, 'No, don't answer at once, I'm afraid you'll say no. Would you think about it?'

'I'd think about it,' Wendy said. That committed her to nothing.

Robbie tightened his arms around her. She felt so good, locked there, close to him. He had never known such bliss.

'Why didn't you leave her years ago?' Wendy asked.

'I suppose I had no strong enough reason,' Robbie said. 'In fact we haven't lived together, as you might say, for years. I've had my own little part of the house, in the attic. We have a few meals together, at weekends mostly. She's often out in the evening seeing to business things or meeting her smart friends. I go on parade with her when it's partners. I can't bear the idea of the new house – I like it where we are. There's a little boy who helps me wash the cars – I do them both on Sundays – and I like the people who run the shop on the corner, and all that. They're all why I've stayed, I suppose.'

Wendy thought it sounded dreadful.

'I don't see any point in staying together because of appearances,' she said.

'I've been lazy, I suppose,' said Robbie. 'That must be why I married her. She's very capable.'

So was Wendy.

He and Wendy had been taken for a married couple wherever they went today. She was wearing a ring – he hadn't asked her about it but was glad; it made it easier at the hotel. He was proud to be seen with her, to have people think they were married.

He wasn't at all proud of being married to Isabel.

12

Isabel had to make her own breakfast on Sunday. By the time she had pattered about in her quilted housecoat assembling it, it seemed hardly worth going back to bed, since she meant to spend the day packing up her clothes and other things for the move the following weekend. Several times she found herself about to speak, to tell Robbie to do something; it was very irritating of him to have gone off like this just now.

She sat at the kitchen table, in the end, eating her toast, while outside on the bird table some puzzled sparrows searched in vain for their morning crumbs. She was sitting there drinking coffee when there was a thump at the back door.

Isabel opened it, and saw Charlie, who took a step backwards at seeing her and not Robbie. His toy pistol was thrust into the belt supporting his jeans. Isabel did not notice it.

'I'm here – where's Robbie?' he asked. 'It's a nice day, we can put some polish on.' Last week it had been agreed that it was time for this on one car, anyway.

'Mr Robinson isn't here,' said Isabel. 'And we're moving next weekend. You're not to come again,' and she shut the door in Charlie's face.

Quick tears sprang into Charlie's eyes as he turned away from the door. Not there – without telling? Something must be wrong. It was true that Robbie's car was not outside but Charlie thought there must be some explanation for that. Maybe it had broken down and was at Monty's Garage round the corner being mended. He ran back home and appeared in front of his mother looking thoroughly dejected.

'Robbie isn't there,' he said. 'And she told me not to come again.'

His mother glanced at her husband.

'Well, they're moving, Charlie,' she said. 'You knew that.'

'Yes, but Robbie's my friend. He wouldn't go away without saying good-bye,' said Charlie.

Charlie's mother decided that the worm had turned at last and Robbie had gone for good.

'Sometimes things happen that can't be helped,' she said. 'I'm sure he meant to.'

Isabel forgot the child as soon as she closed the door upon him. That was one thing that was going to stop: she wasn't going to have a lot of snotty-nosed little brats round at the new house, for Robbie's entertainment. She finished her breakfast and went up to have her bath.

Later, Beryl came round to help with the packing. She was glad of Robbie's defection, for it meant she had Isabel to herself; however, it was typical of a man not to be there when he was wanted. Dressed in neat maroon slacks with a suede waistcoat over her polo sweater, she darted about the house helping Isabel go through cupboards. The removal men would pack everything up but Isabel did not want to leave it all to them and meant to take some of her clothes over to the new house herself. She and Beryl began packing them up in polythene bags. Whilst sorting through them, Isabel discarded some and set them aside to be sent to the charity shop in the town. Robbie should take them round on Saturday morning.

They started on the linen cupboard. Sheets and towels

and pillow slips were put into bags and the necks neatly clipped. At eleven o'clock they paused for coffee.

'We're getting on well,' Isabel said. 'You are a help, Beryl. How would I manage without you?'

'You'll never have to do that,' Beryl assured her.

She loved her job in Caprice. She had just enough responsibility; it wasn't total. She liked assisting the bright young women who formed part of the clientele, and she was good at helping older women to choose suitable clothes. Best of all, she liked feeling that she was needed, and by Isabel. Her employer, moving around the kitchen now, was clearly disturbed by Robbie's absence. What would she do if Robbie were dead, wondered Beryl? Would she mind? She was almost missing him now, but that was partly because she counted on him to carry out various duties, and she had worked out a schedule for the move which his irresponsible escapade might upset. Where could he have gone?

Isabel, in a grey Jaeger skirt and sweater, with three strings of silver chains round her neck, moved round the house with deliberation. She never seemed to hurry, unlike Beryl, yet she accomplished a great deal.

For the second week Robbie failed to provide Sunday lunch. The women took steaks from the freezer and Beryl laid the table while Isabel grilled them. There were éclairs, too, and they drank a bottle of burgundy between them. After that, both were flushed and sleepy so they sat down for a while with the fashion magazines.

Later, Isabel decided to go up to Robbie's room.

'Well, I made it,' thought Detective Inspector Thomas as he drew up outside the neat house in a quiet, tree-lined road. His former wife lived in a bigger, better house than the one he had provided, in which their marriage had ended.

The journey by car took two hours, and as he drove along, Thomas had turned over in his mind the curious case of the Blewton bank raid, trying to understand what sort of man had committed the crime. It had the trappings of amateurishness – the toy gun, the obvious disguise, the improvisation over the car.

None of it fitted a pattern set by other recent raids. He thought they were looking for someone either unknown to them, or who had strayed outside his usual field of operations.

Whoever the villain was, he had committed a serious crime and Thomas meant to get him.

He switched off the engine outside the house and blew the horn. After a few minutes the front door opened and the two boys came out, David aged eight and Jonathan, who was six, so named by their mother. They wore new corduroy trousers and lined anoraks over scarlet jerseys, and looked very neat. They came reluctantly down the path looking backwards over their shoulders at the house, and Thomas's heart sank. Always he hoped for the sight of them eagerly running to greet him, but that had stopped a long time ago. They were strangers, and he wondered if he might not serve them better by keeping out of their lives. Their stepfather, as far as he knew, was a decent man who was good to them. He could see his ex-wife standing in the doorway watching them go. She was pregnant. He waved half-heartedly in her direction as he got out of the car and walked towards his sons. He felt nothing towards her now, not love, not anger; it had all gone cold. It seemed so sad.

'Hi,' he said, wanting to stretch out his arms wide to enfold the boys, but you needed co-operation for that.

'Hi,' said David, to be polite.

Jonathan did not speak.

They got into the car and Thomas handed over bags

of sweets, despising himself for the blatant bribery but how else could he hope to break the ice? By the evening he might just have broken through the barrier of the boys' palpable resentment.

It was so difficult to keep them entertained. They'd already been to the museums and parks in the area; he had nowhere ordinary, homelike, to take them; it was too far to go back to Blewton – if they did that, they'd spend most of the day on the road.

He started the car.

'We'll go to the sea,' he said.

The two boys were silent for the first half-hour as Thomas tried to make conversation. Eventually he extracted monosyllabic replies from them about what had gone on at school, avoiding all reference to their mother and their home life, which included a half-sister as well as the one on the way. He did not want to know about all that and wished he need have no further contact with Pat: she represented his failure.

At last Jonathan said, 'I've got a new bike. I can ride it without hands.'

'He didn't want to come today. He wanted to stay at home and ride it,' said David betrayingly. 'Mum said we'd got to, though.'

Thomas wouldn't ask David if he would have preferred to stay at home too: he knew what the answer would be.

But things improved when they reached the coast. It was cold, and the east wind blew mercilessly at them. Thomas made them pull up the hoods of their anoraks. The tide was out, and after walking slowly at first across the sand, suddenly they began to race madly around, glad to stretch after sitting in the car. When two planes from a neighbouring airfield flew low overhead, Jonathan stretched out his arms and began to swoop and swerve in imitation, roaring, and after a few minutes the more aloof David copied him. Thomas produced a ball, and they played with that; then, when they were warmer, they examined pools among the rocks for crabs and shrimps.

He found a café for lunch where they could have hamburgers and chips. He had learned the hard way not to take them to a sea front hotel, all dignity and damask.

After lunch they went to an amusement arcade and spent a lot of money on the machines. Thomas had time to notice the youngsters lounging around waiting for time to pass; there should be better ways of spending it, and he thought that people were happier when they had to work physically just to survive. He must stop bringing the boys to places like this – but what else was there to do in an area where he knew no one?

Next time, despite the journey, he'd take them back to Blewton, and show them the station. They might as well learn about his job. He'd show them the cells and the patrol cars, and they could hear the radio. They might even grow up to be bobbies themselves. What would their mother say to that?

He took them back to the beach and they played with the ball until it was time to have tea. They wanted beans on toast and sausages, and they drank Coke.

Pouring his own tea, Thomas had a sudden thought.

He had told Wendy Lomax that Mrs Helen Jordan had not been badly hurt by the bank robber. He hadn't told her to keep quiet about it, and she might have told someone, so that the news could have spread and the thief might have heard it. That could explain the telephone calls to the hospital ceasing. It supported the theory, arising from the dumping of the stolen money at Overtown, that they were looking for someone local.

Robbie and Wendy rose late on Sunday morning. They had a long luxurious bath, then packed up, paid their bill, and were ready to leave the hotel.

'I like this room,' Robbie said, reluctant to go.

For two nights it had been home, a safe retreat where literally, for him, time had stood still.

'Yes,' Wendy understood what he was thinking as he stood there, his jacket a little crumpled, his tie crooked. She straightened it. He did need looking after. He caught her and kissed her. The wonder of it had not ceased to amaze him.

She thought, almost afraid, it means too much to him. She liked being with him. He was a pleasant companion, and basking in his patent admiration made her feel good. She wondered if she might tire of it, if it would cloy, for Robbie was sometimes dull. But he was good and kind, and that was worth a great deal.

As they drove into the country, to make their way leisurely back to Blewton, stopping for lunch and a walk, perhaps a visit to a stately home, she wondered if she might, in time, marry him. She would like a little house, children. Robbie was not too old to be a father – she did not for a moment believe that cow of a wife of his, about his infertility, and it would be nice to prove her wrong. After Terry, she could not hope to fall in love again – indeed, the very thought of it was exhausting. She might be content with Robbie, expecting very little more than kindness from him. Was that enough?

Robbie felt charged with energy and confidence as he drove through lanes where thick hedges on either side would form screens of green later in the year. How he despised the weak, satellite man who had circled obediently around Isabel for so long. Now it seemed impossible that he had endured her dominance so totally. Let her join forces with her precious Beryl; she'd manage without him perfectly well. A new life lay ahead, with, in the fullness of time, a safe pension from the bank.

It was just as well that Wendy was going away, although he would miss her. He needed a respite – time to come down from the clouds and be practical. In her absence he would find somewhere to live and inquire about the legal process of divorce. Some of the money, though not much, from the sale of 49 Claremont Terrace was rightfully his and he must take steps to obtain it. Isabel would have to take out a bigger mortgage; she could afford it. He felt no obligation towards her. He hated her more every day.

There had been condensation on the windows and windscreen of the car when they started off that morning. Robbie had wiped them all down before they drove off, but the window on Wendy's side had somehow become smeared. When they stopped for petrol, Robbie opened up the bonnet of the car to check the oil and water, and Wendy saw that he would be busy for a few minutes. She opened the glove compartment of the car to take out the cloth she had seen him use. There were some maps in it, and a torch, and something more: right at the back under everything else.

Wendy did not know what made her pull out the old pair of leather gloves but when she looked at them and saw the dark stain across the back of one, she recognized it at once.

She put the gloves back, and everything else, and was sitting apparently composedly in her place when Robbie got into the car.

Eating his Sunday lunch in a hotel, James Jordan decided to forgive his wife for her premarital trespass. He was missing the comforts of home; too much of his life was spent in hotels and restaurants, for as sales manager of his firm he was often at exhibitions or in foreign cities. At weekends he needed to unwind in the comfort of his well-equipped, well-run house. Things must be restored to normal, but he would never be able to trust Helen again.

He had favoured her return to work when the children grew older. She was an intelligent woman, and as long as she did not neglect her family he thought her time might as well be occupied profitably. The money, too, was useful while the children were at the stage of receiving higher education.

He had met Helen at a party, and had thought her attractive and warm; she was. Now he knew why. He was not, as he had supposed, the holder of the key that had unlocked her personality – her sexual personality, he decided was what he meant. It had already been released by another and what should rightfully have been his had been surrendered elsewhere.

James was worried about his daughter, growing up with contemporary freedom and now, at eighteen, in Paris. Goodness knows what she might get up to there, though the family she was with were expected, by him anyway, to supervise her. If she knew what her mother had done as a girl, the chances of Petra remaining chaste for much longer would be slight.

Splitting the home up would not help. Family stability was more important than hurt pride. Besides, there would be talk.

He drove round to his sister-in-law's house and found Helen playing Scrabble with her niece and a young friend. She did not look particularly pleased to see him and he was obliged to go into the garden to help Tim prune the roses.

Isabel opened the door of Robbie's room.

It was so neat inside that it seemed as though no one

used it, and with its white painted furniture it was like a schoolboy's room, Isabel thought. That was what Robbie was: a perpetual schoolboy, with his carpentry and his television thrillers; he thought she did not know what formed most of his viewing but she had long ago noticed the quick changeover of programme when she returned home.

It was lucky he still had a mother, herself, to look after him. He suited her well enough, appearing at her side as a consort when required and seldom about at other times.

His clothes would have to be moved from his cupboard in polythene bags to the new house, where there were built-in cupboards in all the rooms. Isabel laid down a small pile of bags on the bed. She tried the cupboard door and found it locked. How secretive. What could Robbie have to hide?

She opened the top drawer of the chest of drawers. There was a pile of spotless handkerchiefs inside – the Robinsons used the Kleen-Wash Laundry – and some toys: a soldier in battle dress, a puzzle. She recognized them as trophies from cereal packets. The next drawer contained socks, the next vests and pants which were made of white cotton, like a schoolboy's. She opened the bottom drawer. There were some sweaters in it, neatly folded, but something was poking up through their neat folds, disturbing the smooth outline. Isabel felt underneath them; she drew out a plastic carrier bag. It contained a tweed cap, a nylon raincoat, a pair of dark glasses, a red wig and a bushy ginger beard.

There was something else in the drawer under the sweaters. Isabel bent to investigate. It was a pair of women's stockings.

13

Detective Inspector Thomas delivered his children back to their mother soon after six. They were cheerful now, and parted from him with amity though no hugs. Their new corduroy trousers were damp at the ends, and sandy.

'See you again soon,' Thomas said bracingly, and tried not to feel deflated when there was no response. He saw the pattern ahead: he would visit them less and less, perhaps stop coming altogether.

Driving back to Blewton, he switched his mind away from his domestic distress to the case of the bank raider. The radio appeal had produced nothing about the return of the money; nor had the inquiries in Overtown. The man must have been invisible, Thomas thought grimly. Someone must have seen him. Perhaps he made the drop wearing a different disguise, or none at all. They could dress up a constable in similar garb to the robber's original attire and have him parade around, in the hope that someone might be reminded that they had, in fact, seen him. Perhaps the thief would carry out another raid and leave a few clues. Having surrendered that loot, for whatever obscure reason, he might try another raid to recoup. Was it possible that they were looking for a nutter whose plan was to rob banks for kicks and then give back the cash?

He thought again about Wendy Lomax and how she might have remarked that Helen Jordan had not been seriously hurt. He might as well go round and see if she remembered mentioning it to anyone. If she did, it should be possible to trace a chain along which the news had passed, and in that way a possible suspect might emerge.

With the piece of carpet fibre, which was not from the Jordans' Renault, and with the hair from the false beard, they might get him. The fibre could have come from his own car, and though by now he would probably have got rid of the beard and the other items, he might not have been thorough enough and hairs or other traces might be found among his possessions. There was the dust, too, which might be matched.

Thomas turned into the street where Wendy Lomax lived. It had been pleasant drinking coffee in her room. She might offer him some more.

She was out. Thomas sat outside in his car for quite a time, hoping she would return.

The leak might have come from the hospital, he reflected, waiting there. A nurse might have casually talked about Helen Jordan in some bar; or one of the injured woman's friends could have let it out.

In the end, he gave up.

On Sunday evening, Herbert Green told the Overtown police that he had been walking his dog along the streets of Overtown late on Tuesday night. He had seen a man with a beard, wearing a raincoat and a tweed cap, walking along at a brisk rate. He had noticed the man because it wasn't raining and he had thought it strange that he should be wearing the raincoat, which wasn't a warm one but one of those light ones for travelling. And he'd been wearing dark glasses. He hadn't seen the man get out of a car, nor was he near the bank when observed by Mr Green. This was the only definite statement that the Overtown police could produce, and it had not come in answer to the radio appeal, which Mr Green had not heard. He had just seen the plea in the local paper, which he never got around to reading until Sunday, asking for witnesses.

There were several other replies to both appeals, and all had to be thoroughly checked, but none was precise enough to be taken into account.

Mr Green said that his man had a carrier bag in his hand. He showed the Overtown policeman, on a map of the town, just where he was walking at the time.

'Can I help?' came Beryl's voice as she climbed the stairs.

Isabel stood in Robbie's room staring at the things she had found in the drawer. Quickly she thrust them back under the sweaters and pushed the drawer to.

Without waiting for an answer, Beryl came into the room.

'Well,' she said. 'How chaste. No pin-ups of nudes. It's like a monk's cell.'

Jocularity and scorn were Beryl's two ways of reacting to Robbie in his absence. When they met, she was rather embarrassed, particularly as Robbie always treated her with courtesy that seemed to her to be overdone. His bank manners, she supposed. She hadn't been into his room before, and found it stark.

Isabel simply shrugged.

'He's a schoolboy,' she said. 'Look,' and she opened the top drawer to display the soldier and the other toys. 'He gives them to that child he's so friendly with next door,' she added.

Isabel had not understood what she had found. There must be other items – that was why the cupboard was locked. The stockings were the clue; there would be other women's garments. He must have a partner with whom he indulged his horrible fantasies, who wore the beard. It was vile. And Beryl must not find out.

'Shall we pack up his things?' Beryl suggested.

'No. He can do it himself,' said Isabel, and anxious to get Beryl out of the room, added, 'But we might have a look at his shed. There won't be room for all that junk of his at the new house.'

The shed was locked, but that did not hinder Isabel. She fetched a large stone and pounded at the chain. Beryl, watching, was uneasy as she looked at Isabel's expression, frowning, intent, her face flushed, concentrating wholly on what she was doing. Eventually the hook holding the chain to the doorpost gave, splintering away.

'Shouldn't we leave it for him to do?' Beryl timidly suggested. She would never have violated anyone's privacy like this.

'It's locked to keep vandals out, not me,' said Isabel untruthfully as she struck the severing blow.

She burst into the shed, and Beryl followed. On a peg-board before them hung chisels and screwdrivers, spanners and other tools. There was a vice clamped to the work-bench, and a stack of wood, pieces of varying sizes, stood against one wall. More wood was stacked on shelves. In one corner were ranged the gardening tools, and there was a wheelbarrow up-ended in the corner. A mower, covered with a polythene sheet, occupied more space. It was all very neat.

On the bench, upside down, was a nearly complete table. Isabel lifted it down. One leg had yet to be fitted.

'A coffee table,' said Beryl. 'It's going to be lovely when it's done. He is clever, Isabel.'

'It's all rubbish,' Isabel said. 'We must get it out of here. Come along, Beryl, help me.'

She pulled forward the wheelbarrow and began piling into it the sections of plank.

'What are you going to do with it?' asked Beryl, half appalled, wholly amazed, as Isabel, with demoniac fury, loaded the barrow.

'Burn it,' said Isabel.

'But wood like that costs a fortune,' Beryl protested.

'He bought it with my money,' said Isabel shortly. 'Who do you think pays for everything here? He wouldn't have it to spare for nonsense of this sort if it weren't for the shop.'

As she spoke, she tipped another pile of wood into the barrow.

Beryl had heard Isabel say that Robbie's woodworking occupied him at weekends and kept him out of her way. She seemed to have forgotten these advantages now as she picked up the wheelbarrow and strode off down the garden to the spot where Robbie burnt rubbish, and tipped out her load. Beryl had never seen her in such a fury.

'Fetch some newspaper and matches from the house, Beryl,' she ordered. 'You'll find them in the cupboard in the kitchen – by the back door.'

Beryl made a protesting gesture with a hand, but she obeyed.

Isabel made four journeys from the shed to the bonfire site. She piled crumpled newspaper under the wood and she split some with an axe, to make it kindle more easily. Her hands, wielding the axe, were red and strong. Everything was very dry, but she added some paraffin to her pyre, and when it was built, she put a match to it. It flared up in a most satisfactory manner.

As soon as it was going well, Isabel put the coffee table on top of the flames.

They were different gloves, Wendy told herself, gripping her hands together to stop them from shaking as Robbie got back into the car. It's sheer coincidence, she went on in her head: they're very similar – old brown gloves, with a stain across the knuckles. But she could hear herself telling Detective Inspector Thomas that she would know those gloves again anywhere.

Robbie drove on, seeking a pub he had marked down for their lunch where the restaurant was very good. Wendy watched for road signs on their way; she had become their map reader.

He'd have thrown them away – burnt them – somehow got rid of them, if those were the actual gloves, she thought.

They ate roast beef for lunch, and as Wendy looked at Robbie across the table, she tried to imagine him in a wig, dark glasses and a false beard, holding a gun. She could not do it; the whole thing was fantastic.

'You're very quiet, dear,' he said. He found uttering endearments difficult, he was so unused to them, but he called her 'dear' quite a lot now.

'You'll have to be careful not to say that in the bank,' Wendy said.

'Two personalities, that's what I'll have to have,' Robbie said. 'One in the bank, and one when we're alone.'

Two personalities.

A personality that was a kind, unambitious bank clerk, and the personality of a ruthless robber: could they exist together in one man?

There were cases in the paper of men being arrested for various crimes when their wives knew nothing about what had been going on. Major deceptions took place every day, and crimes were committed by people who went about for most of the time looking perfectly ordinary.

Why should he do it, though, if it was Robbie? He

would know that the amount in one till on a Wednesday afternoon wouldn't be great. And he had given the money back – whoever had committed the crime.

If Robbie had robbed the bank, giving back the money and using a toy pistol were the only parts of the deed that seemed in character. He couldn't have done it. She must be wrong.

When he tried to arrange a night for their next meeting, she prevaricated.

'Let's leave it for now, Robbie,' she said, and when he looked bleak added quickly, 'It's been lovely, I've had a wonderful weekend and you're sweet. But please don't pin me down.'

'I'm too old for you,' Robbie said mournfully.

'You aren't at all. You're a darling,' Wendy said, and she meant it. 'But I've got packing to do for the weekend, and – and I'm going out tomorrow night and on Tuesday,' she hastily invented.

He could have walked into the bank in disguise, done the raid, and reappeared in time for his normal lunch hour return. It was possible. He would have had to put the disguise on somewhere – in his own car, perhaps – and then remove it again. Would he have bothered, in that case, to steal the Renault? He wouldn't need it.

But it had been found close by, near the recreation ground. Detective Inspector Thomas had told her that.

She looked at his lined, pale face, the greying hair at the temples, the brown eyes behind his glasses now gazing fondly at her. He was falling in love with her, she knew, and whilst part of her was pleased, the other part sighed with the responsibility of it. She had done that to Terry – loaded him with the burden of a love he did not want and could not cope with. There was always a moment, with these things, where you decided to go on and let the relationship work itself out, one way or the other, or you decided not to and drew back before it was too late and she had not reached the point of no return.

But Robbie was speaking.

'It's over, isn't it?' he said drearily. 'I just know it.'

What if she challenged him – said, 'Robbie, those gloves in the car – you were the robber, weren't you?' She knew he would not suddenly go mad and attack her; he would destroy the gloves, and he would be at her mercy. But suppose she was wrong – that it was just some freak coincidence – all trust between them would be gone, his that she should think such a thing, and hers that she could imagine he might do it.

'No, of course not,' she answered him. 'I'm just going to be busy for the next week, and then I'm going away. And you've got your move.'

She would ask for a transfer. It might all be managed very quickly. Then she need not have it out with him.

Wendy realized that her thinking did not seem to include telling the police what she had discovered. How could she do that to him? No lasting harm had been done: the money was back and Mrs Jordan not badly hurt. Their interlude together had been happy for them both, but Wendy knew that Robbie had not exploited her at all, while she had used him to comfort herself, in the aftermath of her broken romance.

'Well, we'll see how things are after that, then,' said Robbie. He'd rushed her; that was the trouble. When she was back from Scotland, and he was installed in a flat somewhere, he would court her.

Wendy put the gloves out of her mind during the afternoon and set herself to be a good companion as they toured a castle full of suits of armour. They had dinner close to Blewton, and when they stopped outside Wendy's building she took her case from him and kissed his cheek. Even if she was wrong, and he was innocent, something important was lacking between them. Wendy wanted more than patient, defeated Robbie.

And he looked defeated, leaving her.

He drove off with the picture he had bought for her still in the car.

14

Robbie did not go straight home. He called at a pub on the way and sat there until closing time drinking whisky, something he did only on rare occasions such as after an evening spent singing or with Wilfred Hunt. Through his mind, like a film, ran a series of blurred images: the moments of the raid in the bank were so few compared with all those hours spent with Wendy; it was easy to forget them. But he could never forget Wendy, and because of her, he realized just how empty his marriage had been. He had been cheated.

He went home at last. As he got out of the car, not bothering to lock it, he caught a whiff of woodsmoke on the air, as if someone had been having a bonfire, but he paid it no attention. The house was dark; Isabel was not about, which was as well.

He was very tired, and he was a little drunk: so much emotion followed by alcohol had its effect and he reached his room in a daze. He saw a pack of polythene bags on his bed and wondered vaguely how they had got there, but he did not try to work it out. He was barely able to stay awake long enough to take off his clothes.

In the morning there was a thump on his door.

'Aren't you getting up? You'll be late,' came Isabel's voice.

Robbie had never before overslept in all the years of their marriage. Heart thumping, he got out of bed and blundered into his yellow-tiled shower room. His head ached and his mouth seemed full of fur. He stood under the shower, with the water as cool as he could endure it, hoping to revive, and gradually managed to pull himself into some sort of order. Downstairs, coffee was percolating, and Isabel, casting him a wary glance, poured him out a strong cupful, without speaking.

It must be late if she was down and dressed, Robbie thought, glancing at the clock. He'd just about get to the bank on time if he left at once. He gulped the coffee down, scalding his throat.

Isabel decided not to mention the polythene bags left for his packing; he looked awful. He must have been away with whoever his fearful partner was, she supposed. His rebellious weekend had done him no good at all. Well, perhaps he'd learned something and would come to heel again. She'd have to watch him, though; she would not stand for one breath of scandal.

Wendy had not slept well. Once she was in bed, she had begun to think again about the gloves. She tried to remember the day of the robbery, to see if Robbie had done anything unusual, but she had taken his actions so much for granted that she would not really have noticed. She saw him in her mind's eye walking away with his green carrier bag, in which he put shopping, she knew, and carried his lunch. He had been empty-handed when he returned after the raid, when the police were there. But it would have been perfectly normal for him to leave his carrier in the car. She knew he parked near the recreation ground.

It was all circumstantial: except for the gloves.

She ought to telephone Detective Inspector Thomas now, or at latest in the morning, and tell him about the gloves. It could soon be proved whether or not Robbie was guilty; there was the bit of fibre, to start with, from the carpet of a car. She supposed, if he were the raider, he would have got rid of the beard by now, but they might find a hair somewhere.

It couldn't have been Robbie. What possible motive could he have had for doing such a thing? He didn't need money.

At last Wendy fell into a troubled sleep.

As she arrived at the bank she saw Robbie running along the road and she hurried so that they should not meet in the doorway. He came in rather out of breath and Betty Fox teased him.

'Nearly late, Robbie. Well, my – that would be a first,' she said.

Robbie was thinking, one thing at a time: let me take one thing at a time; it's work now, and if I'm not careful I'll make some slip, with my head in this state. Later, I'll think. He managed to smile at Betty and reply tritely that there had to be a first for everything. As the morning went on, his headache eased and some strong instant coffee provided by the typist improved things. By lunch time he was feeling more normal; he had a lot of work to do and habit took over.

'But if matey is local, he might come from anywhere in Blewton – not just close to that branch of the bank, guv,' objected Detective Sergeant Briscoe.

'Right,' said Thomas. 'But let's start near. Everyone in the area would know the bank wouldn't be as busy on half-day closing as through the rest of the week. People working in the other shops would have the afternoon off and time to do the job – and the thief could disappear round the back of the buildings to get into his own place afterwards. Let's ask them all what they were doing at the time of the raid.'

Briscoe sighed.

'Yes, guv,' he agreed.

Thomas looked at the list of bank employees. Those who were in the building at the time of the robbery were above suspicion. Four people were away at lunch at the relevant time, and three of those were women.

Mr Robinson, the first securities clerk, was having his lunch and strolling in the recreation ground. Mr Robinson had been employed by the bank for more than twenty-five years. Mr Robinson had not reached the highest branch of his profession.

'And we'll find out a little more about Mr Gilbert Robinson, aged forty-five, chief securities clerk,' said Thomas.

Briscoe raised his eyebrows.

'Middle-aged. Frustrated, maybe. An up-yours gesture,' said Thomas.

Briscoe went off to make the necessary arrangements.

Just before one a detective constable was sitting in a car in the service road near the bank, pretending to read a newspaper. He saw Robbie emerge, carrying his green carrier bag, and walk along the street. He went into the chemist's shop, a few doors away from the bank, and the plain clothes officer slipped out of his car and into the shop after him. Robbie bought aspirins.

The plain clothes man bought a tin of Elastoplast and hurried off after his quarry who had vanished when he came out on to the pavement. The Copper Kettle was next door, and peering through the window, the officer saw Robbie sitting in there. He returned to his car and ate some sandwiches.

Half an hour later, Robbie came out of the café and went into the supermarket; he left there five minutes later and his carrier bag now clearly contained some shopping that weighed it down. Robbie walked on towards the corner, and the detective followed on foot. He saw Robbie go up to a black 1100 that was parked beside the recreation ground and open the boot. He put his shopping inside. Then he locked the boot and walked away, along the path through the recreation ground.

The car was parked quite close to the public lavatory, and the policeman had been on duty for some hours. He went inside, and as he stood there, mused that the bank employees doubtless had cloakroom facilities of a higher order on their premises.

His gaze flicked across to the cubicles.

After over a week, even public places like this would have been cleaned. The policeman advanced and inspected the cubicles. Porcelain and concrete floor faced him. The cisterns were high, old-fashioned ones with chains.

The place was not busy.

If the thief had used it to change in, there was unlikely to be any evidence now, over a week later. He would note it in his report, however.

He walked out into the daylight and fresh air, and sauntered along the path Robbie had taken. The man was sitting on a bench, gazing into space. Walking past, the policeman thought he looked very dejected.

A few minutes later Robbie stood up and walked back to the bank, arriving just before two. The detective followed, and noted it down.

Robbie went straight home after work that evening. He slowed the car down as he passed Caprice; the shop was closed but the lights were on, which meant that Isabel was still busy. He did not want to find her in the house.

Wendy had behaved towards him, that day, in a perfectly normal manner, the manner that had been custom until just over a week ago. As at the beginning of their affair, he must now, at its end, take his cue from her and must not importune.

He would finish her coffee table. He could still do that for her.

He went into the kitchen and made some tea. His headache, subdued by aspirin, throbbed dully, and he felt exhausted. He had eaten very little lunch in the Copper Kettle – soup and a roll, and coffee, to swallow down his aspirins. Then he had tried to do the crossword but the clues had blurred in front of his eyes and his brain felt clogged. In the end he had given up. He had bought some food for dinner; Isabel might want to eat; he didn't think he would.

He drank two cups of tea, with more aspirins, and then he went out to the shed.

At first he could not believe it. The door was open, and when he went in he saw that his small stock of timber had gone.

Vandals, he thought at first. Hooligan boys from the town must have broken in, thieving. But his tools were all there and so was the mower. Only the wheelbarrow was missing. Then he realized that Wendy's table had disappeared.

Robbie stood in the middle of the shed, bewildered. It must have been hooligans. But there was no mess – no graffiti – nothing had been turned upside down. His mind focused on the missing barrow and he blundered out of the shed to look for it. As he walked down the garden, fists clenched at his sides, he suddenly remembered the smell of bonfire smoke the night before, and now he saw the wheelbarrow, standing beside the spot where he burned rubbish. There was a pile of wood ash on the heap.

He bent down and ruffled his hand in the grey powdery mass, and found three brass screws.

He had screwed the legs of the coffee table in position, for added strength.

It was quite a long time before he realized that Isabel, not hooligan boys, had destroyed his gift for Wendy.

Detective Inspector Thomas rang Wendy's bell at half past six.

When she opened the door, she looked startled to see him, and then, he thought, almost dismayed.

'May I come in a minute, Miss Lomax?' he asked. 'I'd just like a word, if you don't mind. I won't keep you long.'

'Of course.' Wendy stood back, opening the door widely. 'Sit down, Inspector.'

Thomas sat down in the red velvet chair and once again Wendy took the seat opposite him. She looked very tired.

'I came to see you last night, but you were out,' he began.

'Yes. I went away for the weekend,' said Wendy.

And she'd had a rough one, Thomas decided.

'Well, it wasn't urgent,' said Thomas. 'I wondered if you remembered mentioning to anyone – a friend, or maybe your colleagues at work – that Mrs Jordan wasn't badly hurt.'

Wendy remembered immediately that she had told Robbie. She had told him about the hair from the beard being found in the Renault, and the fragment of fibre, too.

'It doesn't matter if you did,' Thomas added quickly. He knew at once by the sudden closed look on her face that she had told someone. 'I didn't ask you to keep it quiet.'

Wendy said nothing.

'I'd better tell you why I want to know,' Thomas

continued, but all his antennae were out now. There was something here. 'The calls to the hospital inquiring about Mrs Jordan stopped after that, before we raised our ban on news about her. That was why we relaxed it, in fact. I'm thinking that you – or maybe a nurse at the hospital – may have mentioned it in the hearing of someone who repeated it, until the information finally reached the man we're after. I think he may be local, because he dropped the money back at a branch of the bank not all that far away.'

'Oh,' said Wendy.

That gruff voice, the one in the bank threatening her, and the odd one on the recording that Thomas had played to her: could that really have been Robbie?

'I may have mentioned it to Mr Robinson,' she said. 'We had dinner together one evening, and we talked about the robbery.'

'I see,' said Thomas.

Mrs Jordan might have died. Robbie should not go unpunished for that. But he might not have done it. If he were innocent, proving it might cause him so much trouble, and it seemed to Wendy that he had enough, with his marriage, without more, unless it was deserved.

The police would get there in the end if he were guilty, wouldn't they? Without more help?

15

For the first time in her life, Isabel was afraid. A wig and stockings made sense of a sort: drag gear. It was known that men dressed up as women. But a beard did not match up with that idea, despite how she explained it to herself.

It was some time before she would admit the real meaning of her find.

Robbie couldn't have robbed the bank. It just wasn't in him to do such a thing. For one thing, he was fond of it, although he felt he had been treated badly in the promotional sphere. Isabel didn't blame the bank for that; Robbie wasn't worth promoting. To think when she married him that she thought she was making herself secure. Well, there would be a pension, but she made enough in the shop to snap her fingers at that.

Whoever had robbed the bank had returned the money. That was like Robbie. And whoever had robbed the bank had made a mess of things, running down that woman. That, too, was like Robbie.

At lunch time she went home, and went again to his room. His bed was unmade and there was a heap of dirty clothes in a corner. She wrinkled her nose in disgust. He'd been late home and late going to work; all his behaviour lately had been untypical. On impulse she picked up his soiled shirt from the floor and sniffed it, then his pyjama jacket. There was nothing unusual about them; the faint odour of clean male flesh could just be discerned. Isabel noticed his dressing gown amid the muddle of dishevelled sheets and she pulled it out.

A definite scent arose from it: feminine, unmistakeable, from Dior: she smelled it often enough in the shop, assisting customers in the changing rooms.

Robbie had been with a woman over the weekend.

He must have taken the money so that he could spend it on her, his fancy woman, then lost his nerve and returned it.

Blinding rage filled Isabel as she flung the dressing gown down. She did not want Robbie in any sexual way; she never had; she had merely endured that for the first months of their marriage, then pushed him away so that he very soon ceased to want it. Had he been doing this all along? Had women all through the years? He'd never been off with one before, that was certain, but now he was at an age when men, always foolish in Isabel's view, often behaved stupidly.

Isabel did not intend to be the object of pity in Harbington. Robbie was going off with no woman. She opened the bottom drawer of the chest of drawers and took out the objects she had seen the day before: the wig, the beard, the cap and the dark glasses – and the stockings. Fool, leaving them here where they could be found if by any chance the police did suspect him. He was so incompetent he might have left other clues around, and he was so stupid that he might think returning the money would wipe out his crime so that the police would abandon the task of trying to solve it.

It was no good putting the things out with the garbage, and there wasn't time, now, to burn them. Isabel picked up one of the polythene bags she had left in the room for Robbie and stuffed them into it. It was transparent, and the red hair of the wig looked very bright to her as she carried the package downstairs.

She took it out to the car and put it under the front seat to deal with later; she could not leave it in the back for all to see.

Charlie's mother saw a man in a short leather jacket at the door of 49 Claremont Terrace during the afternoon.

She did not go to tell him that Mr and Mrs Robinson were both out; he might be a burglar. But Detective Sergeant Briscoe rang her doorbell and asked where Mrs Robinson was, showing her his identification.

Charlie's mother explained that Isabel would be at Caprice. While they talked, the toy pistol was on the table behind her. Briscoe saw it but made no comment; there were plenty of such toys about. He drove into town, to the shop.

Men seldom entered the premises of Caprice, except at Christmas; very few accompanied their wives on shopping sprees. Isabel sailed forward to greet this intruder who did not look like a customer.

'Detective Sergeant Briscoe, Blewton CID,' he said showing her his card. 'Could I have a word with you, Mrs Robinson?'

Silently Isabel led the way out to the back, behind the shop, where there was a kitchenette and cloakroom and a flat-topped desk where she kept business papers.

Briscoe confirmed that Isabel was, indeed, the wife of Gilbert Robinson who worked at the Blewton bank which had been raided twelve days earlier.

'Has your husband been ill lately?' Briscoe inquired.

'No,' replied Isabel.

'Has he acted strangely?'

'No, not at all.' The lie came instantly.

'Where was he on the evening of Tuesday last week?'

'Tuesday – Tuesday?' Isabel frowned. 'I don't remember,' she said, and was going to add that the detective had better ask Robbie himself, when warnings sounded in her head. The detective would trap Robbie. At the same time she remembered that the first and third Tuesdays in the month were choral group nights. 'Wait!' she exclaimed, though Briscoe was going nowhere. 'It was his choir evening.'

'He'd be late in, then?' Briscoe asked.

'He always goes to the Crown, afterwards,' Isabel said. 'I don't know what time he came in.'

'He was at home this weekend?' asked Briscoe.

'No.' It was useless to lie if the lie could so easily be proved. The man had only to ask that wretched little boy next door if Robbie was at home. 'He was away,' Isabel admitted. She thought of the woman's scent that had clung to his dressing gown. Her lips primmed. 'Visiting friends,' she said.

'The address, Mrs Robinson?'

'Why do you want to know?' Isabel asked.

'We think he may be able to help us establish the identity of the bank robber,' said Briscoe smoothly. Thomas's latest instructions had been to put the frighteners on; no more. He reckoned he'd done it by now.

'Well, I know nothing about that,' said Isabel firmly. 'Better ask the people who saw the robber. My husband didn't. He was at lunch.'

Any last hopes of Robbie's innocence left Isabel as she spoke. He had done the raid in his lunch hour and had thought he'd get away with it. Well, it still needed to be proved.

'Thank you, Mrs Robinson.' Briscoe decided he'd got enough. She'd go back home and tell her husband what had happened, and he'd get rattled. That was what the guvnor hoped for. Better move in, Briscoe thought, with a warrant. They'd find something, if this was matey.

'What did he want?' Isabel's assistant wanted to know when Briscoe had gone.

'Oh, some nonsense about security,' said Isabel.

'From Blewton?'

'Harbington comes under Blewton,' said Isabel.

For once she was totally out of her depth. The police force was not something to be tackled lightly. Isabel knew that a wife need not give evidence against her husband in law. She would not send Robbie down; she would do a great deal to save him, to prevent scandal; and after that, from gratitude, he would be even more surely in her power. There would be no more women.

She still could not believe that there had been one at all, despite the evidence.

She took her time packing up the shop at the end of the day. She liked it then, empty of customers. The cleaning woman came in, and Isabel watched her vacuum round, then dust. Once a week the counter tops were polished. Isabel ran her hand along the row of dresses that hung all down one side of the shop; silks and cottons for spring, and light wools for cooler days; polyester and nylon for easy care; she stocked them all. If Robbie was caught, she would survive; people would be sorry for her. But she did not want pity; she had earned her own security, and from Robbie she wanted the appearance of respectability. She would go to some lengths to preserve it.

Robbie's impulse after discovering Isabel's bonfire had been to retaliate. He had wanted to storm round the house pulling all her possessions out of cupboards and drawers and set fire to the lot.

He went up to his own room. Usually the first thing he did when he came home was to go upstairs and change out of his business suit into slacks and a sweater, but this evening he had gone straight out to the workshop after his two cups of tea.

He had forgotten that this morning he had rushed out to work without making his bed and tidying up.

Robbie sat down on the unmade bed and put his aching head between his hands. He rocked to and fro like a child needing comfort. Bloody woman Isabel: no words that Robbie knew were bad enough for her. He cursed her aloud, using them all.

After a while he got up and slowly began to put the room to rights. When the bed was made he collected up his dirty clothes from the corner where they lay; he might as well put them in the linen basket. His eye fell on the heap of polythene bags which he had not noticed before. How had they got there?

He realized that Isabel had been into his room, and he understood that the bags were for his packing.

She'd burned his wood and the table for Wendy. What else had she done?

Robbie opened the drawers of the chest quickly, one after the other. The toys were there, the soldier and the other things for Charlie. But the wig and the rest of his disguise had gone.

Isabel knew.

He looked at his watch. She'd be home soon.

Robbie took his keys out of his pocket and opened the door of his cupboard. He felt at the back of it. The gun was still there: so her prying curiosity hadn't discovered all his secrets.

He took it out, then felt in the shoe for the cartridges. He loaded both barrels; then he slipped the others into his pocket in case he needed an extra one or two to finish the job.

He decided to wait for her in her bedroom.

Robbie heard Isabel's car. She revved the engine before switching it off. Then came the sound of the door banging. Now she would be walking towards the house.

She always came upstairs promptly, either to change if she was going out, or to do things to her face and put on a different pair of shoes. Sometimes she called in at the office downstairs on the way, if she had brought papers or samples home. She depended on him to produce food for the evening meal, even if he no longer always cooked hers. If she went into the kitchen now she would see his shopping in the refrigerator: chops, though there were probably plenty left in the freezer. He wondered irrelevantly how she planned to move the freezer and its contents. Well, she'd be doing none of that now. He tightened his grip on the gun and stood up, moving over to stand behind the door so that she should not see him when she entered.

He heard her heavy footsteps on the stairs. Then the door opened and she walked in, setting a parcel down on her bed. She stood up, her back to him.

Robbie raised the gun to his shoulder. He was trembling. He had only to pull the trigger and she would be gone for ever. He could not miss her. The barrel of the gun was only a few feet from her back.

Before he could do it, Isabel turned. She took an instinctive step backwards and came up against the bed. If she retreated further, she would collapse upon it. Robbie's face was intent, one eye closed as he peered down the length of the gun. It wavered in his grasp.

'What on earth are you doing, Robbie?' Isabel's voice was steady, but this was a nightmare.

'I hate you,' Robbie croaked. 'I'm going to kill you.' He took a step forward. The end of the gun was inches from Isabel's chest now. 'You burned Wendy's table. You spoil everything.'

'Robbie, you're being very foolish,' Isabel said. 'You don't want to go to prison, do you? You will, if you shoot me.'

'I don't care,' said Robbie. 'You're hideous. You're too evil to live.'

'You're the evil one, Robbie. Who robbed the bank?'

But Robbie didn't care about the bank now.

'You said it was my fault about the children. That we hadn't any. It wasn't. It was your fault. That was very wicked of you, Isabel.'

Isabel was very strong, and she brought her right arm up fast. It caught the barrel of the gun and knocked it sideways.

The sound of the explosion was deafening.

16

Ten minutes later the doorbell rang.

Isabel glanced out of the window. She could see Charlie's father standing on the doorstep. She went downstairs and opened the door to him and said 'Yes?' inquiringly.

'Oh – is everything all right? I heard a noise – it seems silly – it sounded like a shot,' said the young man rather awkwardly.

Things next door had been strange for some days. There were the late arrivals at night – or rather, in the small hours – and Charlie's return in tears on Sunday morning after Mrs Robinson's harsh dismissal. Charlie and his parents always thought of Isabel as Mrs Robinson, but Robbie was Robbie to them all. Then there had been Mrs Robinson's bonfire on Sunday afternoon; she had been seen putting a table on the fire – old rubbish, probably, being turned out before the move, but Charlie's parents had never seen her working in the garden or lighting a fire before: all such jobs were Robbie's.

'It was the boiler you heard,' said Isabel smoothly. 'Some sort of backfire. It will have to be attended to. I've turned it off.'

'Oh, I see,' said Charlie's father, feeling foolish.

'Kind of you to call,' said Isabel in a grim voice. 'Wait, will you? Robbie has some things for your little boy.' She moved back into the hall and called upstairs, 'Robbie? It's Mr Pearce from next door. You've got those toys.

Shall I come and fetch them?' She paused. 'He may not be able to hear me,' she said. 'He's lying down. He isn't feeling very well. I'll just fetch them. We're moving on Saturday, and Robbie wants – er – Charlie to have them before we go. Wait a minute.'

She did not invite him in. Charlie's father stood on the doorstep while Isabel ascended the staircase in a majestic, unhurried manner. She was gone only a few minutes, returning with the soldier and the other toys that had been in Robbie's top drawer.

'Thanks very much,' said the young man. 'Charlie will come and thank Robbie himself before you go.'

Isabel closed the door upon her caller and looked at the clock: five minutes to seven. Charlie's father would remember that she had been speaking to Robbie at that time.

When the gun went off, Robbie had fallen to the ground. Isabel had snatched the gun from him and stood it against the wall, well away from him. For all she knew it might go off again. She looked at Robbie who was trying to stand up, moaning slightly and holding his hands to his eyes. She saw that the shot had buried itself in the wall, low down near the skirting board.

Robbie cringed away from her.

'You're ill, Robbie,' Isabel told him in her normal stern voice. 'Come along upstairs.'

She took him by the arm and pulled him to his feet. Robbie allowed himself to be half led, half supported, up the stairs to his own room where he collapsed on the bed, curling up, knees to chin, in a helpless posture.

Isabel looked at him with scorn. Her mind was moving fast. She went down to the bathroom and took four tablets from her bottle of sleeping pills. They were Mogadon and looked like aspirin. She rarely needed them but kept them for the few times, such as sales weeks, when she felt overstimulated and sleep was elusive. She took them upstairs, with a glass of water, and made Robbie drink them down.

'They'll do your headache good,' she told him. 'You've got one, haven't you?'

Robbie nodded. He was scarcely aware of her actions. At this moment, Charlie's father called, and when Isabel returned to Robbie's room to fetch the toys he was lying with his eyes closed, almost drowsing.

After Charlie's father had gone, Isabel took a glass from the kitchen. She put on the rubber gloves she kept by the sink and polished the glass well. Then she filled it with whisky. Back in Robbie's room again, she dissolved more sleeping pills in the glass while he lay there, eyes closed, moaning a little. She did not think they were very strong pills and they might not be enough for her purpose: she would have to embellish her plan, and her eye had fallen on the polythene bags so conveniently waiting.

She put an arm round Robbie's shoulders and raised his head.

'Drink this, Robbie. It will do you good,' she said, and held the glass, cloudy with the drug, to his lips. 'It's whisky,' she added, as he grimaced.

Robbie was too far gone to protest at the taste. He drank the mixture, Isabel making him hold the glass, and when it was all gone she put it down on the floor beside the bed, then tipped it over on its side, for realism. She had brought the bottle of pills up with her, and she pressed his fingers round it, then set it on his chest of drawers.

She waited a few minutes, until he seemed to be asleep, before she slipped one of the polythene bags over his head and shoulders. It ballooned with his breath. She took a tie from his drawer and secured it around his neck to prevent oxygen entering. She had read of such suicides. She lifted Robbie's hands and pressed them to the bag in case the shiny surface retained prints, then laid them down again.

She took away the bathroom glass and returned it to its place, washing and polishing it. The police would assume that after she had gone out, Robbie had come downstairs and helped himself to the whisky and the pills.

She must, therefore, go out.

First she went out to the car and brought in the bag containing Robbie's pathetic disguise. She put the items back in the drawer where she had found them. There was no way of telling how much time she had: the policeman who had come to the shop that afternoon might decide to call.

She intended to say that after she got home that evening, she had heard a sound like a shot from upstairs. She had found Robbie in her room, lying on the floor with a gun beside him. She had moved it from his reach, and he had muttered something about the raid on the bank but she hadn't been able to make sense of what he was saying.

She might be asked if she thought he had tried to shoot himself, and she would reply that she supposed he had. He had been behaving strangely lately.

But she had told the policeman that afternoon that he had not been acting strangely. She would have to say that naturally she had said that: her husband's behaviour was a private matter. She would never have imagined he could be responsible for the bank robbery, but of course it explained everything, she would add. If only she'd known.

She had already planned to go out for the evening, and when Robbie was lying down she had gone ahead, she would say. She might be criticized for this.

'You mean you left your husband alone in the house after he'd tried to shoot himself? And with the gun still in the house?' she imagined herself being asked.

'I didn't know what to do,' she would reply. 'I wanted to talk it over with a friend. And I wasn't late home.'

She dare not be late: this could not be left till the

morning, it would seem too callous. She would look in on Robbie after she returned and would discover his weird suicide. He must have thought it the only thing to do after robbing the bank, she would say, and wondered if she would manage to squeeze out a tear.

She put the rubber gloves back in the kitchen. Then she telephoned Beryl, who was overjoyed at the opportunity to offer her supper unexpectedly, although it would have to be somewhat scratch at such short notice.

'Something rather upsetting has happened, Beryl,' Isabel said. 'Robbie isn't at all well. I want to talk to you about it.'

She would have to ask Beryl to say that their evening together had been prearranged: it will make it easier, she would say, and Beryl would gladly agree to that small deceit. She'd tell Beryl the version of the shooting that the police would hear later; it would be a good chance to rehearse.

There was no more to be done. Isabel left the house, locking Robbie in; for all she knew, he was already dead.

Detective Inspector Thomas rang Wendy's bell at eight o'clock the next morning. He had been up for most of the night.

Wendy was dressed, and eating Weetabix. She knew at once that something more had happened, and stood back silently to let Thomas into the room.

He seemed unable to begin what he came to say, so Wendy offered him coffee, which he accepted, but he set the cup down without drinking any. This was going to be even harder than he had expected.

'Miss Lomax – Wendy,' he began. 'I've got some very bad news.'

An icy feeling filled the pit of Wendy's stomach. Robbie

had been arrested. But it wasn't her fault, she told herself quickly; she'd told no one about the gloves.

'It's Robbie,' she said.

'I'm afraid so,' said Thomas, and added, 'I'm very sorry, he's dead.'

For an instant Wendy stared at him.

'No!' she said. 'No! He can't be!'

'I'm afraid he is,' said Thomas.

'But – but the bank raid – ?' Wendy put her hands to her mouth, aghast.

'He did it.' Thomas said. 'We were just beginning to catch up with him. Had you guessed? The phone calls?'

'I knew,' said Wendy, almost whispering. 'But not till Sunday. It was the gloves – they were in his car, in the locker. He didn't know I'd seen them.' She sat down and folded her arms across her body as if to comfort herself. 'I know I should have told you,' she said. 'But I just couldn't.'

That terrible woman, Mrs Robinson, had said that her husband had been away for the weekend but that she did not know where he had gone. So he'd been with Wendy. What a toil, thought Thomas wearily.

'But how did he die?' Wendy asked, and then answered her own question. 'He must have killed himself.'

'No,' said Thomas. No need for Wendy to be told now that it looked as if Robbie had tried to kill his wife, though Mrs Robinson insisted he had tried to shoot himself; when this failed, he had tried another method, she maintained.

'He was murdered,' said Thomas. They'd be charging her this morning.

'Murdered?' Wendy stared at him, horrified, her face white.

'An attempt was made to make it seem like suicide,' said Thomas.

He thought of Isabel Robinson's hysterical raving in

the night. The Harbington inspector had called him when he discovered that the dead man had worked at the bank which had been robbed. Mrs Robinson had said that a detective from Blewton had been to her shop in the afternoon, inquiring about her husband. She said she had no idea that he was involved with the robbery, but her prints had been found on the dark glasses in the drawer. She'd lied a good deal, it seemed, and her lies about the shooting were not clever: the angle of the shot in the bedroom for instance, did not look like a suicide's aim, and there were spare cartridges in the dead man's pockets. Suicides didn't expect to miss. She could have only one reason for not telling the police what had really happened with the gun.

In the end, the woman had raged, 'She's not having him, that woman – whoever she is. He's mine,' and had muttered something about 'Wendy's table'. It had taken most of the night to put it all together and there were still some loose ends to tie up. All the things used in the robbery except the toy pistol were in that bleak attic room. A more accomplished villain would have destroyed the evidence, but Robbie hadn't even got rid of the gloves. The pistol might yet turn up, but there was plenty to nail him without it.

'How?' Wendy asked. 'How did she do it?' For it had to be Isabel who had killed poor Robbie.

'Sleeping pills,' said Thomas. 'And whisky. He wouldn't have known anything.'

Wendy could learn later about the polythene bag. At first the Harbington CID had thought they'd got an accidental death, a sad man breathing carbon monoxide for kicks and going too far. But the woman had hurried to tell them about the bank and the disgrace if Robbie were charged with the robbery. They'd got on to her then, quite fast.

'Poor Robbie,' said Wendy again. 'He was so unhappy.'

'Not all the time, surely?' said Thomas curtly. He'd had a pretty good weekend, for instance, with this girl. 'Think about the good bits,' he advised, and added, 'You won't be involved.' Not if he could help it.

'He knew we weren't going on together,' Wendy was saying. 'He was very miserable on Sunday night, when we parted.'

Thomas felt his heart lightening at this news.

'It had nothing to do with you,' he said. 'His wife found the things he'd used for the raid – his disguise. She didn't want the publicity of his arrest and trial. But she wasn't quite clever enough.'

There had been none of his prints on the bathroom cabinet, where the medicines were kept. It was difficult to see how he had fetched the bottle without leaving some trace of his visit to the bathroom, which was so clean and well polished that it bore no signs of his presence in it at all.

The Harbington inspector had been disgusted. To him, the only bright aspect of the whole case was that one of their mysteries had been solved: a missing shotgun had turned up. They hadn't begun to find out how Robbie had acquired it.

'People like this, with everything they can want,' the Harbington man had said. 'How can they do such things?'

'We both know it happens all the time,' Thomas had answered.

'She murdered his soul first,' said Wendy slowly, looking at Thomas at last. 'Over all those years they were to-gether.'

'Yes,' Thomas said. 'People do that to one another. Look – have some coffee. I'll make you a fresh cup. And mine's gone cold, too.' He bustled about, preparing it, then sat opposite her among the remains of her breakfast. 'Drink it up,' he said.

'I should be going to work, I'll be late,' said Wendy.

'Never mind about that,' said Thomas. 'Look – couldn't you go away for a few days? What about that friend of yours, the one where we went for the pistol? Could you stay there for a bit? Till the fuss has died down?'

If she was around, she might be questioned; the super might insist, when he saw the report. But she wasn't an essential witness. The press would like her angle, though, and might uncover the whole story.

'I'm going to Scotland on Saturday to stay with my mother,' said Wendy.

'Could you go today?' Thomas asked.

'My holiday doesn't start until Saturday,' Wendy said.

'I think we might arrange something with the bank,' said Thomas. He'd already had a talk with the manager, upon whom he had called before coming here, rousing him before his alarm clock had rung. Nigel could not believe that quiet, dependable Robbie had robbed his own bank and had met such a dreadful fate, and kept wondering what head office would have to say about the disgrace.

Thomas looked at Wendy. He'd have to take it very gently.

'When you come back,' he said in a light voice, 'maybe you'd help me fix up a picnic for my two lads. I'm not much good at that sort of thing.'